Praise for Jenna Bayley-Burke's *Her Cinderella Complex*

"This is a fantastic story with very strong characters who were beautifully written and I immediately fell in love with both of them."

~ *The Good, The Bad, and the Unread*

"Her Cinderella Complex was a wonderfully sexy and fun book...Their sexual encounters were extremely erotic...Her Cinderella Complex is the first book that I have read by Ms. Bayley-Burke and it won't be the last."

~ *The Romance Studio*

"Her Cinderella Complex is a delightful gem that had me laughing out loud and rooting for these two people to make it. Just when I'd think I had the plot figured out the author, Jenna Bayley-Burke would throw me a curve, which kept me on my toes, and interested in finding out what happened next! ...This is a fast-paced book that will not only have you smiling but enjoying the hot, steamy and sometime funny love scenes. At no point does the story drag. So do yourself a favor and treat yourself to having a good time while reading Her Cinderella Complex ."

~ *Literary Nymphs*

"... a marvelous book that I enjoyed from start to finish and it portrayed characters that were down to earth and that I could really relate to. Ms. Bayley-Burke is an author I love to read and this book will definitely go into my keeper collection."

~ *eCataRomance*

"The characters were splendid and jumped off the pages. The whole concept of the story was very intriguing and was enough to keep me glued to the pages until I finished the book. Would this happen in the real world? It would be very nice if it did and I was Heather. The sexual tension was exactly where it needed to be."

~ *Fallen Angel Reviews*

Look for these titles by

Jenna Bayley-Burke

Now Available:

Par for the Course

Her Cinderella Complex

Jenna Bayley-Burke

A Samhain Publishing, Ltd. publication.

Samhain Publishing, Ltd.
577 Mulberry Street, Suite 1520
Macon, GA 31201
www.samhainpublishing.com

Her Cinderella Complex

Print ISBN: 978-1-60504-013-4
Digital ISBN: 1-59998-472-5

Editing by Imogen Howson
Cover by Scott Carpenter

First Samhain Publishing, Ltd. electronic publication: February 2008
First Samhain Publishing, Ltd. print publication: December 2008

Dedication

For Cherry Adair and everyone at the Emerald City Writers Conference who finished the damned book.

Chapter One

"You're late."

Heather Tindall stared at the back of the tremendous leather office chair. Since it just barked at her, she assumed someone sat there, but it was too big to be sure.

Wiping her damp palms against her black skirt, she took a deep breath. The temporary agency had warned her Golden City's CEO burned through executive assistants daily. She got a full day's pay no matter how long he kept her. So far, no one had made it to their coffee break. Heather had no intention of kowtowing to someone who would fire her within the hour.

"Your clock's off. My agency was told eight, and according to my watch I'm thirty-two seconds early."

The black chair turned slowly, revealing the most gorgeous man she'd seen off a movie screen. Deep brown hair, a strong uncompromising jaw, and black-fringed eyes that sparkled a surprising aquamarine. She'd expected a crotchety old man, not someone from the pages of a magazine. Her pulse jackhammered as a sloppy smile played on her lips. Too bad he didn't have the same response.

"You think that's funny?"

Oh damn. She'd make the record for being fired the fastest. She cleared her throat. "Where would you like me to start?"

"I don't know. It's your job, not mine." He spoke with a mocking slowness that made her wonder if he was teasing, or truly an ass.

"There's a desk in front of your office door. I'm guessing that would belong to your assistant."

"It did until two months ago when she retired."

"She didn't train someone before she left?" He must have run her off too.

"There was no time. Her daughter adopted triplets, and if anyone can schedule three babies, it is Carla."

"She's not coming back?"

He raised a straight eyebrow. "I've seen them. They're cuter than me."

Heather smiled, doubting looks had anything to do with it. He wasn't cute by any means. Handsome, jaw-dropping, mouth-watering. Heather sucked in a cooling breath and dragged her mind out of the gutter.

"And you have no idea what it is she did for you." Which was why he was so short with the parade of assistants who'd been through the revolving door.

"Not the first clue." The sensual promise of his smile surprised her.

She pushed her wire-rimmed glasses tighter against her face, reminding herself men like him did not look at girls like her that way. He probably dated models and debutantes. Her last boyfriend had been a house painter.

"I'll check out the desk and see what I can decipher."

"Don't bother. You're not what I need."

He turned to his computer and began to work. Heather blinked and checked her watch. She'd been fired after one minute on the job. That had to be a record, and not one she had any intention of making. She'd never been fired before, and no matter how handsome this clown was, he wasn't breaking her streak.

With a shake of her head she turned on her heel, making sure to close the door behind her. She didn't even want this job. The temp agency hoped she could mollify him until they found the ideal candidate for the job, and found her the event-planning position they promised three months ago.

She had a marketing degree for goodness' sakes. Not that she'd used it yet, but she had ideas brewing for corporate events that would wow someone, anyone, if they cared to give someone without job experience an interview. Darned recession.

With a huff of breath, Heather plopped down into the adjustable desk chair and surveyed the mess that lay in stark contrast to the pristine office. Curtis Frye's inner sanctum was decorated in the same style as the other two floors of Golden City Property Development offices she had been led through like a lamb to the slaughter. Everything echoed money and success, from the black leather armchairs to the Ansel Adams prints in heavy black frames on the walls. With as many walls as were in this company, she guessed they'd bought every photograph the man had ever taken.

They shouldn't have bothered with the art—the view was breathtaking. From this high up in San Francisco's financial district, you could see all the buildings in town. Working late would become a treat. The skyline lit up would make it worth the extra time.

Just like the other desks she'd seen, chrome and glass stretched before her now. Terribly ineffective. No one could hide chocolate in this place. Pushing her feet against the thick charcoal carpet, she propelled herself towards the bank of black filing cabinets, staying seated as she tugged on the drawers.

The bottom one opened, empty save for a black binder labeled *Duties*.

With a sigh of relief, Heather dropped her purse inside the cabinet and lifted the binder. Either Frye's assistant didn't do much, or she was so busy she didn't have time to type up more than the single-spaced page outlining all the things required before Mr. Frye's eight a.m. conference call. *Good night!* She'd been getting up mighty early if she'd had to do all that.

Still, it was better than being unemployed. With no other way to make rent in too-expensive San Francisco than to accept the temp jobs, Heather had learned a thing or three about adapting quickly.

The desk was piled high with memos and files, random faxes and reports. Thanks to her parents' real estate company back home, she knew the basics of the business. By the time her stomach growled she'd sorted everything, and round-filed most of it. From the metallic cup holding pens atop the desk, she procured the key to the filing cabinets, and took care of everything but the few items she was unsure if Mr. Frye had cared enough to cast his eyes on.

"What have you done?" His tone was as harsh as a whip, stinging her pride. She turned to see him looming over the desk, his face tight with irritation.

"You're welcome." Heather smiled brightly at him.

His dark brows shot up as he straightened. Her smile widened. This was a man who needed to be taken down a few pegs.

"I'm going to head out for my lunch hour. I'll tackle the computer when I get back." Rolling back to the filing cabinets, she retrieved her purse, then stood.

Curtis Frye stood between her desk and the door to the outer office. For an instant she thought about trying to run around the other side of the desk to get past him, but decided he needed to prove he was worth her efforts.

"Why are you still here?" he said through gritted teeth.

"You called the agency and said you needed help. Voila!" Heather lifted her arm like a spokesmodel selling a sedan.

"I told you to go. You'll be paid for your time."

"About that," she started brightly. "You can't fire me, since you never actually hired me. If the agency is going to pay me for a day's work, I'll do the work."

He glanced over her shoulder at the clean desk. "What did you do with everything?"

"Filed it, except for these." She handed him the papers. "I noticed you usually initial memos before they are filed, so I held these back."

He leafed through them, his eyes widening as he read one. "This is a month old!"

Heather bit back the smart reply she was itching to give him. She'd made her point.

With a huff, he leaned across the desk, plucking a pen from the cup to initial the memos. Heather's mouth went dry at the sheer proximity of him, terribly aware of his intense masculinity.

She gave herself a mental shake. This would not do. She'd never been attracted to someone she worked with before. Taking him up on his offer to fire her would put her out of the misery of working with him and never having him give her the time of day. She opened her mouth to tell him she wouldn't be coming back, but before she could utter a sound he straightened up and spoke.

"You really want to be my secretary?"

Jolly holly sticks, did people really use that term anymore?

"Personal assistant."

He had the nerve to roll his eyes. "You really want to be my personal assistant?"

"No. I want to be an event planner, but nothing like that has come up." Which was why she'd spent the summer since she graduated jumping from job to job every week, covering vacations for a multitude of different careers while she sent out résumés.

His lips tilted in a grin. "Are you always this honest?"

"Of course. If you play games, someone has to be the loser. Better to say what you mean."

"I don't think you are right for this job."

Heather nodded, glad she'd set a record by making it to lunch. And the next person who came in would have a better shot since the desk had been cleared.

"You'll stay on until I find someone with experience, or until you find your event-planning job. Agreed?" He held out his hand for her.

Her palm slid against his, his thumb making her skin tingle as it closed over her hand to squeeze in affirmation. Sensations whirled through her like a hurricane, her insides quaking so hard she could barely manage to shake his hand. He relaxed his grip, slipping from her grasp.

"It's settled then. I'll see you after lunch." He turned, marched back to his office and closed his door.

Heather wilted, grabbing the chair for support. If she reacted this way to a simple touch, she really should refuse the offer; walk away before someone got hurt. Like her.

Curtis stared at the résumé the agency had faxed over, trying to do the math to figure out whether his new assistant was even legal to drink. He needed someone with enough life experience not to be rattled by the unexpected, and they sent him an adolescent.

Maybe. She could be as much as twenty-two. Damned discrimination laws obliged him not to ask. Little Miss Sunshine certainly took to the paperwork quickly, and she had tenacity. He needed someone dedicated, hardworking, and above all trustworthy. Young people had a tendency to say more than they needed to, and that could blow a deal. He winced—he was thinking like a man twice his age.

Curtis heaved a heavy sigh, tossing the fax into the trash. She'd bail soon enough. Most of the workload of his assistant had been parceled out to the rest of the support staff. Once she had the full picture of the duties required, she wouldn't be so eager. But in the meantime, she'd earned her chance. Anyone that determined deserved a fair shake.

Curtis lifted the phone from its cradle and punched in the numbers for the staffing agency, telling them Heather would stay on until they found him someone with actual experience. He hung up knowing when they found a better candidate, he'd be able to give Heather a job in the Human Resources department here at Golden. They could use someone to plan corporate events and take the burden off the rest of the department.

Whether she opted out or he moved her to another department, she wouldn't work for him long. Couldn't. She set him off-kilter, looked at him in a way that wasn't entirely appropriate and yet was completely innocent. He had a knack for knowing how people would react before they did, but she'd completely surprised him today. He did not like surprises.

Once Heather got things sorted, she found the systems were well organized and it only took her a few weeks to get Curtis Frye's life back to normal. The rest of the administrative team eased her into her position, handing tasks back one at a time. As she went, she finished writing the manual his last assistant had started. Hopefully it would keep him from having to go through a blip like this again.

Within a few months she knew everything about him. Which newspapers he took—she separated out the front page and business section for him to read on the treadmill, how he liked his coffee—Americano every hour from eight until noon. Lunch was delivered then, soup in paper cups so he could drink without having to stop working.

The job of his executive assistant was to do everything to make sure he could work as much as possible. She learned more personal information about him than she knew about another person. She paid his bills, so knew his Social Security number and birthday. Learning he was a Gemini cleared up so many things.

Curtis was actually his middle name, but she never asked him why he'd ditched a nice name like Jason. His clothes were ordered every season, but Heather did have to trek down to Needless Markups with his credit card to pick up his wardrobe. The lot of it barely fit in her compact sedan.

A hairstylist came every three weeks and did something to his hair during a conference call with his partners in New York, but she never knew what. His hair always looked exactly the same. The day-to-day matters of his life took a back seat to his business.

He didn't take a moment for himself, but he did make time for others. Every month, his mother phoned in charity events he needed to attend, and to schedule the family dinner. He'd rescheduled a meeting in Prague just so he could have dinner with his parents.

Her parents had been so impressed she was working for Golden City and Curtis Frye. *He's brilliant,* they told her. Shrewd, aggressive, insightful, sure to be one of the biggest real estate moguls the country had ever known by the end of the decade. *But at what cost?*

By the time the employment agency came through with the event-planning job she'd waited for, she'd already appointed herself in charge of making sure Curtis Frye was taken care of. Not just his coffee, suits and travel arrangements. She tried to get him to play more golf, telling him it was a great way to network when she really wanted him to have the stress relief of the exercise. She arranged for him to have no meetings on his birthday. Granted, he used the day to catch up on paperwork, but he went home in the daylight, with a smile on his face.

So it struck her as odd when, six months after she came to work for him, he called her to his office and asked her not to take the event-planning position she'd been offered. He didn't volunteer how he knew she'd been offered another job.

"I know your degree is in marketing, and you've been waiting for a position with an event-planning firm. But I'd like for you to work for me, not the agency. That way you'll be eligible for profit sharing at the end of the year."

"That would be nice." She drew a circle in the lush carpet with the toe of her boot. She knew she should tell him she'd already turned down the position, but he wasn't big on thank-yous, or any conversation at all really, and she liked being appreciated.

"I agree. That way we can double your salary and lease you a car for errands."

She plopped down into the leather chair opposite his desk. "Excuse me?"

"We couldn't do the car until you were a Golden employee. It's an insurance nightmare."

"You're doubling my salary and giving me a car?" She brushed a wayward wisp of brown hair from her face and tucked it behind her ear.

Heather wore her giddy smile, the one where her tongue poked from between her teeth. Her features seemed too large for her face until she smiled, then everything came together perfectly. She looked like she'd won the lottery.

"Leasing. I'm sorry you're so shocked. I must not have done a very good job of communicating how much I recognize the value of what you've done these last few months. You're a fantastic assistant, and I want to make sure you stay with Golden."

She blinked, her green eyes glazing over behind her thick glasses. Her nose and mouth wouldn't seem so large if the lenses didn't shrink her eyes. Always keeping her long hair pulled back in a barrette at the nape of her neck didn't help either.

Curtis clenched his fists beneath his desk. It did not matter what his assistant looked like, nor what she could look like if she tried. She was terrific at making his life easier, and she was one of the few people who'd earned his trust by passing small tests he'd given her with credit cards and sensitive business information. If he gave her enough, maybe she wouldn't sell him out the way everyone else did.

"I know changing your career plans is a sacrifice, but you will be compensated accordingly."

"I don't know what to say."

Neither did he, and things were getting a tad uncomfortable. "It's Friday, so you could say, see you first thing Monday morning."

"Except you'll be in Los Angeles on Monday. You fly out Sunday at two. The tickets are in your portfolio. Your housekeeper has your bag packed and the town car has been ordered to pick you up."

"Is there anything you haven't thought of?"

Heather popped up from her chair, smoothing her hands down her black trousers. She always wore black. Her cheeks tightened as she tried not to smile. "I haven't thought what kind of car I'll lease."

The email caught Curtis's attention, sending his guard up. The staffing agency was confused: Heather had arranged to extend her assignment, and he'd asked to have her employment transferred to Golden City. After a short phone call, he learned Heather had declined the event-planning job he thought he'd need to bribe her out of the day *before* he made his offer.

Omissions were the first sign a person couldn't be trusted. He needed to confront her, gauge her reaction, and odds on find another assistant. *Just great.*

A few more phone calls, a handful of favors he'd have to repay later, and his meetings were all moved to San Francisco for the week. Annoying as all-get-out, but he'd know by Monday morning if he'd be back on the executive-assistant merry-go-round.

That should have settled things, but he couldn't tamp down

the feeling of betrayal. This was business, not personal, and yet he hated thinking he'd been wrong about her. The sooner he found out the truth, the better.

Acid bit at Heather's stomach as the elevator climbed the floors to the office. All weekend she'd felt horrible. The low-level hum of guilt she'd felt when leaving the office on Friday had intensified every hour until she was sure she'd go crazy before Curtis returned on Wednesday.

She'd lied. Not complete perjury, a white lie really. Still, dishonesty made her uncomfortable. Her sisters made fun of how even secrets like who was having a party or cheated on a test weren't safe with her. It hadn't made her popular in school, which left her planning the dances instead of attending them, but she'd told herself she didn't mind so long as she was involved. She'd grown up in a small town, where everyone knew everyone else from the sandbox and dating was darned near incestuous anyway, so she'd waited to find her Prince Charming when she made it to university in the city.

But school had been filled with men prone to take advantage of her honesty, rather than appreciate it. She'd been as lonely there as she'd been at home, until she'd moved into an apartment with two culinary students. Fantastic friends, but their companionship showed on her hips. She dressed completely in black, which she hoped was slimming. Keeping her wardrobe monochromatic was cheaper, for sure.

Heather took off her glasses and rubbed the tension from her eyes as the elevator dinged. She made her way off the lift and straight into the last person she expected to see.

"Mr. Frye!"

"Miss Tindall." His gaze cut her as sharp as a scalpel.

"What are you doing here?" Heather struggled with her glasses, missing her ear the first time.

"I work here." The chill in his voice made her shudder.

"No, I mean, in the office. You have meetings in Los Angeles."

"I moved them. Will you come to my office, please?"

Head down, she followed him, laying her purse on her desk as she went. Nothing good ever came from lying. Omitting. Whatever. Which was why she never did it. Until Friday when she got greedy with her need for his attention.

The tears started before she even sat down. The hot wash of frustration and fear flooded her cheeks, and she couldn't do anything to make it stop. Some women had a feminine cry, but Heather had seen herself in a mirror mid-fit and she knew what she looked like. Red runny nose, pink puffy eyes, splotchy face. She took off her glasses and pressed the palms of her hands against her eyes, hoping the pressure would stop the flow like it would on a wound.

It was no wonder Curtis Frye never saw her, no man ever saw her. She was a mess. An anxious bundle of nerves and rules, and look at that—black smudges on her hands from the mascara she wore to try and make her eyes show up through the distorted curve of her glasses.

"I'm going to have to ask you to stop crying." Curtis held out a box of tissues. She plucked a few out, doing her best to clean herself up.

"I'm sorry."

"Yes, well. I don't know what to do with tears. I didn't—I mean, I only asked you to come to my office."

Heather shook her head. "Good granny, this is not going

well."

"I agree." He crossed his arms over his chest and leaned back against the edge of his desk.

She looked up at his face, the tense set of his jaw, the worried look in his eye. She should have taken the other job. Staying here was pure torture. Working this closely with a man she'd fallen more for every day, who couldn't even see her...it was pathetic.

"I lied to you. On Friday." She sniffled, trying to get over the tears and through this conversation with some modicum of dignity. "I let you think I was taking the event-planning job when I had already decided to stay on here. It was a mistake." She let out a deep breath, not feeling half as relieved as she expected to.

He blinked, uncrossing his arms and setting his hands beside him on the desk. "I'm not sure what to say."

"I shouldn't work here."

"Excuse me?" His eyes flickered, brightening.

"Something's happened, personally, that's changed the way I'm acting professionally. It's best if the agency finds a replacement." Her stomach ached and her eyes felt heavy again.

"Is it me?"

"No, you're perfect." *I'm the one who is messing everything up.*

"Then we'll reassign whoever it is that is upsetting you."

"No." Her words were barely more than a whisper. To get out of this one she'd have to lie, again. Even white lies snowballed.

"It's not a problem. I have associates in other cities. I can call in a favor. Give me a name and it will be taken care of."

He pulled another tissue from the box and handed it to her.

Her pulse jumped when their fingers brushed.

"I was going to ask you about why you didn't tell me you'd declined the other job offer, and you outed yourself. I admire that kind of honesty. You're the best assistant I've ever had, and I'll do anything I need to keep you with me."

If only he meant *with me*, the way she wanted to be with him. "Still—"

"Do you like working with me?"

"Very much." There was that honesty kick again, kicking her in the butt.

"Then give me his name. It will be handled by the end of the day."

"Frye!" A voice boomed from the doorway. "What is wrong with the weather in this town! How can you people claim to live in California, when I need a sweater in summer?"

"Alan, come in." Curtis ushered in his first meeting, while mouthing the words *we're not done* to Heather.

Chapter Two

Never had an email made her happier. In the name of keeping her mind off the conversation she'd need to have with Curtis, she'd managed to organize his entire week perfectly, so his note to pick up lunch came as a relief. A grin lifted her cheeks. If he was so busy in his meeting with casino developer Alan Morgan he couldn't use the intercom, he might not have time to finish what they'd started. *Fantastic.*

Calling ahead to the caterer who normally delivered, she ordered six different box lunches. That way they'd have a selection, and she could leave at a decent hour and they'd only have to open the refrigerator in Curtis's office for their dinner break. The caterer offered to deliver, but Heather desperately needed to get away from the office to think.

There was no way out of the hole she'd dug. She couldn't give Curtis a name. No matter what he said, office romances were never thought of well. Being responsible for a black mark on someone else's career was simply impossible.

It wasn't like she could tell Curtis she had a hopeless crush on *him.* The reason faced her as she stood waiting for the elevator, her reflection staring at her in the shiny metal. She'd seen the women Curtis dated. In newspapers and magazines. She lived her life trying to avoid being one of those fashion don'ts in magazines. They just didn't mesh anywhere outside her fantasies.

Not that she thought herself ugly. She was neat, well put-together. There were a lot worse things than having a big nose and full lips. The door dinged and she stepped into the elevator, the air heady with the mingling perfumes of the two women already inside.

She recognized them as working for the public relations firm two floors above Golden. Heather admired every single woman who worked there, wished she could pull off the chocolatey wrap dress with the leather sandals and beaded necklace, or the plum tweed blazer with matching ruffled-hem skirt. Occasionally she'd try outfits like those on, but they never made her look like the women in the elevator.

She stifled the little voice that wondered if that was the real reason she'd chosen to stay here with Curtis rather than make the jump into the world of event planning. The basic black she always wore was completely acceptable, especially from a man who did not see you as a woman, but someone expected to bring in new clients and instill confidence that every party would be a great time might need to look the part. And she looked...dependable.

Not that there's anything wrong with that.

By the time the doors dinged open she'd decided she'd earned whipped cream on her blended caramel iced mocha. There was only so much introspection a girl could handle in the presence of perfect specimens like the PR mavens and Curtis without caffeine and sugar in high doses.

The deli that handled the catering was happy to make her mocha a triple, and even threw in a sampling of all their cookies for good measure. Heather didn't have the heart to tell them Curtis didn't eat cookies. He seemed to have a ban on all things that did not make his body function more efficiently, poor soul.

The walk back to the office was much too short. Since moving to San Francisco, Heather often lost track of time while out walking, ending up at her destination before she realized it. She lost herself in the mismatched Victorian and Art Deco buildings, relishing the beauty in their differences.

Every weekend she could manage, she signed up for a walking tour through one of the neighborhoods—Chinatown, Telegraph Hill, Cow Hollow. Each neighborhood as big as the town she grew up in, still holding its individuality and quirky history while gleaning the benefits from being part of something bigger.

The walk through the financial district came to an abrupt halt outside her office building. A news van was stationed directly outside the front door, blocking the entrance. As she maneuvered her way inside, she caught snippets of conversation between the reporter from the news van and the security guard instructing him to move the van or it would be towed.

"Ten To Watch..."

"...magazine..."

"...only one this year..."

"...never happened before..."

"...national coverage..."

The entire building was abuzz with whatever was going on, and all she could think of as she rode the elevator up was finishing her mocha before she made it to her desk. Once she was inside her office, there was no place to hide anything. She'd locked the outer door when she left to ensure he had privacy for his meeting, so she could pitch it at the reception desk, as long as she finished. She didn't want him to think she'd been dawdling while running errands.

"That's his secretary," she heard through half-open elevator doors.

"Executive assistant." Wasn't there some national movement to abolish that term? She stepped to the reception desk, narrowing her eyes at the dozen or so people standing there. Reception was a formality at Golden. No one ever waited there.

"Where is he?" asked the peanut gallery. It would have been fine if it were in unison. But they all said some variation of it at once. What horrid noise.

"I'm sorry, what is this about?" Heather asked Pam, the receptionist.

"You haven't heard the news, have you?" Pam looked as giddy as a schoolgirl.

"News?"

"About Mr. Frye?"

She arched a brow, not wanting to play *ask me another.*

"The Times named him their Ten To Watch."

Heather nodded. "They did that last year."

"Yes, but this year he's all ten."

She pressed her mouth into a line to keep from looking surprised and giving the reporters something to work with. They wanted to unsettle his normally poised and polished self by ambushing him with the news. The media hunted him ruthlessly for one reason or another, hoping to find a chink in his perfection. There had to be a way to give him time to prepare. She cleared her throat.

"You did tell them he has meetings scheduled in Los Angeles this week, didn't you?" Curtis had been there when she arrived, at least an hour before Pam. Maybe she didn't know he'd changed his plans.

"They don't believe me."

Heather took a deep breath. She had to throw them off his trail. Since working for Curtis she'd witnessed firsthand the way the media hounded him. The way publicists called to arrange dinner dates so he could be photographed with starlets after he was named one of the fifty sexiest men, and when he made the most eligible bachelor list it wasn't only the media that went after him. Once his picture was in the paper, people thought his privacy was up for grabs. For a person as private as Curtis Frye, Heather could only imagine the toll that took.

She'd stressed him out enough with her lying debacle, causing him to move meetings that would have kept him safe from this, or at least given him some warning before the onslaught. It might not be her fault the vultures were circling, but she'd be darned if she'd shine a light on their prey.

Turning to the crowd, she plastered on a smile. "Is there something we can help you with?"

"Is Mr. Frye here?" a bottle blonde asked.

"Do you think I'd be shopping on my lunch hour if he were?" She held up the brown-handled bag, thankful the caterer used plain bags.

"Where is he now?"

"He had meetings scheduled in Los Angeles through mid-week." So far, so good.

"Is he aware of the *Times* honor?" Hello Mr. Pink Hair. Got to love San Francisco.

"You'll have to ask his publicist."

The click of the lock on the office door at the end of the hall vibrated down her spine, yet she was the only one who seemed to notice. "If you'll excuse me."

She didn't wait for an answer, just made a not-so-graceful beeline for the office door, blocking her body in front of it the second it opened, knocking Curtis to the ground before she slammed it shut and locked it once more.

"Well, look at that!" Alan Morgan said from the doorway of Curtis's office. "She knocked you clean off your feet."

"I'm so sorry, Mr. Frye. It's just—"

Curtis held up a finger, silencing her immediately. He propped himself up on his elbow and glanced at Alan. "Can you give us a moment?"

"But my blood sugar—"

"Take the bag with you." He looked back at Heather, her eyes wide. She best not start crying again. "Lunch *is* in there, right?" She nodded and Alan grabbed the bag, retreating to the office and thankfully shutting the door behind him.

Heather knelt next to him on the floor, biting her full bottom lip. "You can't leave right now."

Curtis sat up, stretching his long legs in front of him and shook his head at the incredulity of the situation. He'd been bowled over by his assistant who probably weighed about half of what he did, and now she wanted to hold him hostage in their office. Not that he planned on leaving since she'd brought in what he was going out after, but still. This day was showing him Heather Tindall in a whole new light, and he hated to think how much he liked it.

"I'm not going anywhere. But you can't knock people down, Heather. Someone could sue me." He smiled, but she didn't catch the joke, just nodded furiously. Odd, since she usually had a great sense of humor. That, and her willingness to try, had been the first things he'd liked about her.

As the weeks turned into months he'd valued her more, not just for the way she efficiently managed his days, but because no one ever had a bad thing to say about her. Office politics never swung someone's way that whole-heartedly. She was a study in contradiction—efficient yet slightly silly, quick-witted and sharp-tongued, yet eager to please.

She stared at the floor, her lips pursed, eyes closed, her heavy wire-rimmed glasses pressing on her nose. How he'd hated wearing glasses, the way they'd controlled his life. Having them knocked off and not being able to see his hand in front of his face as a kid, not being able to leave in the morning before he'd gotten his contacts in as an adult. Heather should see the doctor who did his eye surgery three years ago. It was the most freeing experience. He opened his mouth to offer, but a knock at the door caught their attention.

"Stand behind the door," she ordered with the authority of a drill sergeant during basic training.

"Excuse me?" Curtis asked as he rose. He did not take too lightly to being ordered around by anyone. And still, his feet walked his body to the far side of the doorway.

"I'll explain as soon as they're gone." She pulled open the door slightly.

"There's a problem. Heather," a vaguely familiar voice whispered. "His car is in the garage."

"It's mine," Heather replied smoothly. "He's leasing me a car as part of the position now that I'm hired on. He wants something flashier."

"Flashier than a Jaguar?"

"I just say, yes sir." The smile came through in Heather's voice.

"Okay, I'll let them know."

Heather closed the door, then leaned back against it, her hand on her stomach. "Why couldn't you have driven the SUV today?" She shook her head. "I need your keys."

"You want my car?" Curtis pulled them from his pocket and handed them to her. He didn't need a repeat performance of this morning's emotional explosion. Besides, he could take them back once he had some answers. "Start talking."

Her hand formed a fist around his key ring. "You were named *The Times'* 'Ten To Watch' today. Reporters have infested the building like hornets at a barbecue. I think I've thrown them off, but we'll have to wait and see."

Curtis couldn't help but laugh. "You make a horrible bodyguard. Protecting me from paparazzi while knocking me to the ground in my own office." Finally, she grinned. "I'm going to go convince Morgan he needs in on the New Orleans rebuilding projects. This will all blow over by the end of the day. It did last year."

He closed his office door without hearing Heather explain that last year he wasn't all ten.

Heather Tindall listened to country music. Loud country music. When Curtis had emerged from his meeting this evening he found a note, a bag, and a car key from Heather.

He'd thought she was handling the media like some covert operative, instructing him to put on the sweatshirt and hat he found in the bag and drive her car home. But in the parking garage he realized she wasn't exaggerating, much.

Three paparazzi photographers were hanging out on the executive floor where his car would have been. Bile bit the back of his throat as his steps quickened to the safety of Heather's Honda. He was a hunted animal, and he didn't understand why there was a target on his back.

Trying to think about what was happening, maneuver

through traffic, and work Heather's stereo took up the entire drive home. It wasn't until he was in his driveway that he realized he had no way to get into his garage—the garage door opener was in the Jag.

As if by magic the door went up, Heather standing inside next to the Jaguar. With a deep exhale, he shut off the car and climbed out. He stepped to her, frustrated, hunted and needing answers.

"Start talking."

Heather wrinkled her nose, a forced smile on her lips. "No wonder you don't wear hats. You have an enormous head. It's not something anyone would notice until you put a baseball cap on, but in the future I'll find a different kind."

"Heather—" he growled through gritted teeth.

"I don't want the Jaguar. I can't handle a stick shift with all the hills. I didn't think anyone in San Francisco had a manual transmission. Besides, it's not exactly the kind of car you get for your assistant to run errands."

"Are you amusing yourself? Because I'm not laughing. I had to drive home in disguise, had paparazzi waiting in the parking garage, and I don't know why. I'm sure you know exactly what is going on. So unless you tell me right now, you're fired."

"Touchy. I told you. *The Times* named you their 'Ten To Watch'."

"They did that last year, and it was my publicist's problem, not mine."

"Oh, she's bamboozled, not to worry. She also thinks you're in LA. I've had lots of messages to have you call her as soon as you get back because she has interviews scheduled. Television and print. Wait until you see your Friday agenda." She let out a long, low whistle.

As glad as he was Heather was back to her bubbly self, he needed to know what was going on. “This is your last warning.”

“You are *The Times’* Ten To Watch.”

“But what is all the fuss about?”

“You are all ten.” She counted on her fingers. “Your New York housing initiative, New Orleans rebuilding project, Las Vegas casino, the Chicago high-rise, the Portland transit project, the mentoring program at Willamette University you spearheaded that is producing top-notch MBA students, and some others that were less flattering.”

He winced. “Less flattering?”

She cleared her throat. “Your networking abilities with the daughters of hoteliers and Greek shipping magnates were listed.”

Damn. He couldn’t be in negotiations with anyone who had an attractive daughter without the press assuming he was negotiating a bedmate instead of a business deal. Why was everything he did tainted by some playboy rumor? Why couldn’t he be taken seriously based on his accomplishments?

“Do you want me to clear tomorrow so you have some time to prepare for this, or batten down the hatches because you’ll be coming in?”

“Business as usual. Publicity doesn’t get in the way of a deal.” Curtis nodded his head and checked his watch. Past ten. Much too late to invite Heather in.

“See you in the morning then.” Heather held out his keys, exchanging them for hers. She nodded at the garage door. “You should go inside, in case someone is out there.”

He didn’t like that idea one bit, letting her go out there alone, when the mercenary paparazzi could be about, so he could cower behind a door.

"I want to make sure you get into your car safely."

"But what if they get a picture?"

He pulled off the hat, running his hand over his hair. "Then I'll look like I work too hard."

The scent of roses wafting through the house meant everyone must have heard about the magazine before he did. Making his way to the living room, he saw the reason for the perfume.

Roses were everywhere, looking extremely out of place in the wood and leather sitting room. The inlaid walnut cocktail and end tables were made to stand plain, not be covered in flower arrangements. The dark brown of the leather sofas made the bright whites and greens pop to life.

The Frye family always sent roses for any occasion. He knew he was lucky to have such a supportive family behind him, but the roses always reminded him that they only looked out of place here, not at any of the other Frye children's homes. But then, this was more of a house than a home.

The phone rang and his back stiffened. Would it be the press hounding him as the clock ticked towards midnight? Couldn't they ever leave a person alone?

He reached for the extension, but heard his housekeeper, Mrs. Rutledge's, voice answer from somewhere in the house. Before he could appreciate the reprieve, she appeared in the hallway, the phone tucked between her ear and shoulder as she hefted an oversize arrangement of lilies.

He took the arrangement and set it on the only available space, on top of the tin-paneled armoire housing the television.

When he turned back to Mrs. Rutledge, she had the phone in her hand and a sad look on her soft face.

"Congratulations." Her smile was weak. She knew him so well. "Would you like me to have the flowers taken to the Veterans Hospital or the Alzheimer's Center?"

"Whose turn is it?"

"I split them when you won that Sexiest Man thing."

"Should we split them again, then? There seems to be enough."

Mrs. Rutledge nodded. "You are such a generous man, Jason. Your mother would be proud of that."

Curtis smiled. Mrs. Rutledge had lived next door to his parents before it all went bad, was his only connection to a mother he hardly knew and barely remembered. "And what about this Ten To Watch business?"

"Oh, I think she'd be as overwhelmed by it as you are." A genuine grin made him want to ask her to sit down, talk with him about anything besides the latest projects he had running or his publicity nightmare of a life.

She held out the phone. "Kendra is on hold. She claims to know you are not in Los Angeles. Heather thought it would be best if I let everyone think you had gone on the trip, but Kendra..." She rolled her eyes. "I hope she is a wonderful publicist because her personal skills are lacking."

"Thanks for trying to hold her off." Curtis took the phone, watching Mrs. Rutledge walk away with his chances of having a normal conversation. Not that he had many. Any.

Curtis Frye did not have time to waste on idle chatter. Jason Curtis was the one who was lonely, and he needed to get over it.

He clicked on the phone, deciding it was better to deal with

Kendra sooner rather than later. After all, dealing with the media circus was what he paid her for.

"I don't have time for interviews on Friday." Best to let her know up front he wasn't letting her work this for more than he had to.

"Heather's taken care of that. We need to strike while the iron is hot. Do you think you have a book in you? All you need is the idea, a premise, and we could get a ghostwriter-"

"No book. No interviews. Reporters are disrupting my business. You know nothing gets in the way of my work. Make them go away."

She followed up her shrill laugh with a snort. "You're hot. Enjoy it, Curtis. Milk it. It's not going anywhere as long as you are single, successful, and savvy. Oh, I should write that down." He heard the rustle of paper, the scratch of a pen. "Unless you plan on tanking your career or marrying some boring twit and ducking out of the singles scene, you are front and center for the duration."

"I'm not in the singles scene." He hadn't had a relationship since Lindsay, the decorator he'd hired to furnish the house, realized he wasn't really a Frye.

"Please. You're handsome and available, you only need to be seen in the same restaurant as a celebrity and you're engaged. It makes my job easy."

"Let's make it harder. No press this week."

"Curtis, really. You're being unreasonable. This is a huge honor. Your father really worked to make sure you were on that list."

"John made this happen?" He shook his head. He should have known. John Frye would pull any string to get his children further ahead. Scholarships, school admissions, internships, interviews, recognition—he took personal pride in their every accomplishment.

"He wanted you on the list again, and the editor-in-chief of *The Times* is a golfing buddy of his. You made all ten. They want the publicity of this too, so declining interviews is a slap in the face to them, and your father."

Right. She worked the guilt angle well. Which was why pictures of him with debutantes he could barely name graced the society pages and rumors of relationships with actresses he'd hardly met ran rife through social circles he avoided like the Ebola virus.

John Frye wanted him to be a success. Truly, being successful was the least he could do to repay the man who'd given him a chance at life. A real life.

"Kendra, it's late. I'm tired. Heather will call you with the interviews I'll have to postpone." He clicked off before she could argue, then turned the ringer off the phone. No doubt she'd try calling back. Tenacity made her great at what she did, but annoying when you needed to get away from her.

There was nowhere he could go to escape from it. The New Orleans restructuring deals were too important for him to put off while he hid out somewhere else and waited for it all to blow over. He had to show up and shoulder the stress of the media hounding him. Maybe he could even use the attention to bring more investors into the project. Something good had to come of this.

He trekked up the stairs to the master suite, a room as big as his entire house before he came to live with the Fryes.

Lindsay, the designer the Fryes used on their vacation home in Malibu, had shown him so many options, and he'd thought she'd known him as she selected things to his liking. Everything had seemed to fit his idea of what the house should look like. Masculine. Rich. Warm.

She missed the last one by a mile. Especially in the bedroom. He laughed to himself at his own joke. The last woman he'd taken to bed had been cold, had wanted to be part of a family he was only a guest in, and as soon as she learned the truth she'd set off for bluer blood.

Just as well. He hadn't needed the personal detour and it was best things ended before she rejected him and not his lack of lineage.

Maybe her frozen inner core chose the décor of the room. He hadn't had a chance to ask. The room had been set up after she'd gone, leaving him alone in a sea of black and white.

Discarding his clothes into the hamper, he set to work on the piles of pillows on the bed. Even going to sleep was a chore in this room. Each pillow zoomed toward the white chaise he'd never sat on, the different patterns of black-and-white chunks of fabric landing mostly where he planned.

From the microfiber bedspread to the black headboard to the curtains everything matched, and he hated black. The only color Jason Curtis Sr. would allow either of them to wear after his mother died. People thought it chic, classic, but to him it represented death and the darkest period of his life. A loss so deep it had turned his cop father into a drug addict, then dealer, then taken him all together.

Curtis climbed beneath the sheets and tried not to think about those years, about how a man who respected the law had twisted it, used it to ease his pain. About paper routes, walking dogs, mowing lawns just to keep food in the house.

When things went sour and his father wound up in prison, it was Mrs. Rutledge who asked her employer, John Frye, to take him in instead of letting him be sucked into foster care. How she convinced them to agree, he still didn't fathom. The Fryes were wonderful, but they'd never taken in children before or after him. He'd simply gotten lucky.

He rolled to his stomach, pulling a pillow beneath his head and wishing for sleep. Maybe in his dreams he'd come up with a way out of the public eye before some reporter dug too deep and wanted to talk about Jason Sr. He'd never been asked before, and if he could get out of the media spotlight, maybe he never would be.

But to get out of the spotlight he'd have to tank his career, which he couldn't do. Way too many people depended on the projects he developed. The Fryes would kill him if he did something to change his appearance. Delia Frye made a career out of her children, and so she took every success personally, including how they looked. It bothered him in junior high, but now that he was busy he appreciated that she ordered his suits every season. The only option left was to attach himself to someone out of the public eye, make himself less of a story and perhaps throw the press a juicier bone to chew on.

He would be successful and look the part, nothing could change that. But Kendra could feed the media a story, give them something sensational to gnaw on and he could get back to work. If his personal life was seen as sewn up tight, then all the articles and accolades would focus on his work. He had no problem talking about his projects, just the personal life that was a front. If someone chiseled hard enough it might crack and hurt people who depended on him. The Fryes first, but like the proverbial snowball, it would gather dirt and momentum as it sped downhill. Investors would question the son of a felon, and God forbid, pull their backing.

Curtis Frye off the market would make a line in gossip columns, and then he'd be done with them for good. Focus on work, on building his career, on being himself instead of on the lookout for the person who wanted to tear away his armor.

His muscles relaxed with the idea. He only needed to find a suitable relationship. That should be simple, right? Women were always complaining they couldn't find a man ready to commit. He'd aisle-walk tomorrow if it meant he could be taken on his own merits. His shoulders bunched again. He'd have to find someone he could trust completely, someone he could depend on, who respected what he wanted to do. Someone like Heather.

The smile came without warning. He'd never thought of Heather much outside of the office. He wondered what she must be like, the dichotomy of spunk and formality she juggled. She wasn't seeing anyone now since her relationship with whomever at the office seemed to have soured.

She was the perfect assistant, and she'd provide the perfect escape.

Chapter Three

Curtis climbed three flights of stairs, all the way to what once must have been the attic of the converted Victorian house. From the single door at the end of every flight, he guessed each floor housed one apartment. At the door he paused to check his watch. Five thirty. He knew Heather got to work sometime during his East Coast conference call, but he had no idea when she left. Or even if she was awake.

Some women took hours to get ready, others no time at all. He didn't think Heather was the type to fuss with time wasters like make-up and hair products, but she never looked disheveled either.

Maybe he should wait downstairs. But then if there was another way out of the building and he missed her...

Oh forget it. He stepped closer to her door, the warm smell of cinnamon and apples lingering in the air. His mouth watered as he knocked.

He straightened his jacket, smoothed his hands on his slacks and tried to relax. When he couldn't, he knocked again.

The door swung open, a stunned-looking Heather standing in the darkened doorway. With her hair wrapped in a lime green towel and wearing a bright orange terry cloth robe trimmed with blue stitching, he almost didn't recognize her. Not to mention that without the glasses her eyes were as large as the other features on her face, bringing everything into balance.

"Close the door," a voice croaked from inside. "It's letting light in."

"Is something wrong?" Heather whispered, glancing nervously at the darkness behind her.

"No, not wrong." Curtis cleared his throat. "I brought the SUV. I thought we could drive in together and then you could keep it."

She blinked, her lashes long and feathery without the distraction of her glasses.

"Heather, please." The voice croaked again. "I have to get some sleep. This isn't fair."

"I'm sorry," she whispered in the darkness. Turning back to Curtis, she looked him up and down. "I just got out of the shower. I need to throw some clothes on."

"And don't burn those turnovers." The voice spoke again, muffled this time.

"Right." Heather nodded, then shook her head with a silent laugh. "Follow me, but be quiet."

He stepped carefully behind her into the dark room, wishing she'd turn on a light. He could barely make out a countertop in what must be the kitchen. Heather moved with stealth precision, not making a sound as she opened the oven, the cinnamon scent intensifying. She shuffled about, but he couldn't tell what she did until she thrust a plate into his hands and walked past him.

He fell in line behind her, not knowing where they were headed until she closed the door after them and turned on a light.

"Carmella worked late last night, and then Stacia's boyfriend is over so she had to sleep on the couch. I'm sorry about bringing you in here. I know it's not terribly professional, but, well..." She sighed and smiled up at him, setting down two steaming mugs. Her hand fingered the towel. "I'm going to get dressed and we can scoot out of here." She pulled out the chair to a pink-painted desk and motioned for him to sit. "Stacia is the pastry chef at Pazzo's. The apple turnovers won't disappoint."

With that she spun into what he guessed was her bathroom, giving him a chance to absorb the reality around him as he sunk into the chair.

Heather was not black and white at all. She was Technicolor. From her bright robe and towel to the gold four-poster bed draped with pink satin and covered in iridescent stripes of raspberry, cherry and cotton candy.

He tried to take in this new version of Heather, wondering if she still fit in his plan. On top of her desk sat two photographs in glittery frames. Heather not long ago in a cap and gown. Somewhere it registered she'd graduated college a little over a year ago, right before coming to work for him. Which might mean she wasn't jaded enough to agree to his plan. But then, she'd also be young enough to start over as a very wealthy woman when their arrangement ended.

Not that he planned on taking no for an answer. Projecting a relationship with Heather to the public was his only way out of the spotlight, and so he'd stop at nothing until he achieved his goal. Just like the other projects he tackled, this would be no different. He'd make sure they both got what they wanted, and the matter would be settled quickly.

Aromas of cinnamon and apple tempted him from the plate. He lifted the warm, flaky turnover and took a bite. The pastry crumbled onto the plate and he leaned forward, careful not to cover the desk and his suit in crumbs. Sweet, gooey apple filling flooded his mouth.

Between bites he pondered the next photo. A little girl, dressed up like a princess complete with tiara and full tulle skirt, stared at him expectantly, her bright green eyes full of innocent hope. Large features and long limbs made the little girl gangly and awkward, except for the expression of total confidence.

"I was Cinderella four years in a row for Halloween." Heather emerged from the bathroom, looking like she did every day. Glasses hiding her eyes, hair pulled tightly back, matching black pinstripe jacket and skirt.

He stood, brushing the nonexistent crumbs from his slacks. "You look nice."

Her cheeks pinked and she bit her bottom lip, reaching for the other turnover. "Thanks for waiting."

"No problem." He lifted the picture frame, smiling at the hopeful girl. "So which one is Cinderella? Someday my prince will come?"

"That's Snow White. Even as a kid I couldn't see the upside of being a maid to seven dirty boys." She cupped her hand beneath the pastry to catch crumbs as she bit into it.

"What was it about Cinderella that got you? Does the prince ride in on a white horse and carry her away?"

"Not exactly." She set down her half-eaten turnover and reached for one of the mugs. Tea by the looks of it. "Besides, I'm not Cinderella. She had ugly stepsisters and an evil stepmother. My sisters are gorgeous, and my mother is a saint who thinks I hung the moon." She sipped her tea and nodded at the other mug. "You should try this tea. Carmella, my roommate from the living room, is the sous chef at Typhoon, and their tea menu is larger than most restaurants' wine list. This is cinnamon vanilla. It makes the pastry taste even better."

His gaze snagged on her full lips as she sipped at the tea. When he caught himself staring he picked up his mug and took a long swallow. Not bad, for tea.

"So what was it about Cinderella?"

Heather shrugged and set the mug down. She made the few steps to the other side of the small room and opened her closet. When she turned back around she held her black purse in one hand and a pair of heels in the other.

"Probably the shoes," she said as she sat down on the bed and slid hers on. "The magic of a fairy godmother annoyed me because it ended at midnight, but the shoes lasted. And the prince took one look at the shoe and knew that was his woman."

Heather stared down at her boring black sling-backs—department store staples, not even knockoffs—and winced. Curtis Frye was in her apartment, in her bedroom, watching her put on her discount clothes and listening to her prattle on about fairy tales. The fact that he'd shown up at the crack of dawn without so much as a word of warning proved all the more he didn't see her at all, just a box labeled *assistant*, not even a person enough to have a life outside of him. It really would be self-preservation to find another job.

"I'll never look at shoes the same again." His voice vibrated through the room, tickling her ear.

She stood up to let him know she was ready, but found herself chest to chest with him, toe to toe. In all the months of working together he'd never come this close to her on purpose. Even when she'd bowled him over, his rigid posture had made her quick to scamper away. But here, in her room, he stood still. Standing there he seemed so much broader, firmer, more sculpted and muscular than even she'd imagined.

This is Curtis Frye, your boss, an annoying voice niggled in the back of her mind, but she refused to listen. Something was different, something had changed. The sea blue gaze on her was warm and inviting and she wanted to dive in, indulge the fantasies she'd been hiding since coming to work for him. She tried to look away, to protect what was left of her resolve not to fall for him completely, but his stare held her so firmly, she couldn't.

"Are you ready?" He reached for her, his hand on her arm, making her skin feel tingly and alive beneath his touch.

She nodded, wondering if he realized all her assent meant. She trembled as they made their way to the door and out of the apartment, no longer in fear or dread that he might learn of her crush, but with heart-pounding excitement that if he did, he'd take full advantage of it, and of her.

The email stated what he wanted. *Dinner. 8. Luxe.*

If only Luxe weren't closed tonight for a private party, Heather could surely get a reservation for Curtis and his dinner companion. Who she really hoped was Walter Landry, the bushy-haired riverboat magnate he'd spent another day locked in his office with.

Curtis preferred long meetings, keeping the conversation going until everyone saw things his way, not giving his business partners a chance to sleep on it and change their minds. He never ended a meeting until all decisions weighed in his favor, playing upon people's vanity like a concert pianist. Everyone who left his office thought they had swindled him into a deal that was too good to be true.

Usually it made Heather want to laugh, the way such powerful people were so skillfully played, made her proud to work for a man who knew what he wanted and made it happen. Except today it felt like a manipulation, because she might be on the receiving end of his fortitude. He wanted something from her, but what?

Her fingernails scratched at the tops of the computer keys, trying to think of how to phrase *pick another restaurant.* She hated to disappoint him, especially today.

Since he'd shown up unexpectedly at her door in the predawn hours of the morning, his entire demeanor towards her had changed. Completely.

On the way to the office he'd driven to a coffee kiosk, then ordered his Americano and a blended iced mocha for her without asking her what she drank.

She rarely took a coffee break, only when chocolate and caffeine were an absolute necessity for sanity, and then she hoped he hadn't noticed the plastic cup in her trash. But she should have known his razor-sharp mind missed nothing. Even things she'd rather he forget.

After he'd parked the SUV in his reserved spot, he hopped out and rounded the car so fast he managed to open her door before she could do it herself. His hand on her elbow as she climbed down, on the small of her back as they walked to the elevator, ignited her imagination.

She hadn't known what to say when he handed her the keys. The meek thank you seemed totally inept. The entire situation felt...otherworldly. As if a real-live fairy godmother had waved her magic wand, said *bibbety-bobbety-boo* and *poof*...Curtis Frye saw her as a woman.

Only to take it all away again with the chiming of the elevator doors.

As soon as they left the elevator he was all business, dialing into his conference call and changing his clothes. By the time she made it into his office he was already on the treadmill, his lean body hidden behind the latest sweat-wicking fabric, the tailored Italian suit hanging on the back of the bathroom door. She set the newspapers on the table at his side, his eyes already glued to CNN, reading the closed captioning as he talked investments with his New York cohorts.

She'd been invisible to him again an hour later when she announced the arrival of Walter Landry. When she delivered coffee to them, Curtis hadn't so much as looked at her.

So it was no wonder she felt as if she'd spent too long on a Tilt-a-Whirl, at once thrilled at his attentions and dizzy with the worry it could all be in her head.

She typed out the message about dinner, then hit send with a tinge of regret. She'd hoped to work late tonight, wait for Landry to leave and then thank him for allowing her to take over the lease on the SUV, rather than have to hunt for a car and wonder what would be considered practical for an assistant who needed to run errands. It wasn't the SUV worth her annual salary, that's for sure.

Her email beeped.

Dinner. 8. Luxe.

Brows knit together, she stared at the screen. Just how did he expect her to make that happen?

With a huff she fingered through her Rolodex and picked up the phone. In a few minutes Curtis Frye had dinner reservations at three of the best restaurants in San Francisco. Everyone had a table for the current talk of the town.

Heather emailed him the restaurants he had to choose from and hit send with more force than was necessary.

In a few seconds his reply made her eyebrow twitch.

Good idea.

No telling her which restaurant he selected so she could cancel the others, just *good idea.*

Whatever that meant. This day definitely called for plentiful quantities of caffeine and chocolate, preferably blended together.

"Are you ready?"

Heather jumped in her seat, adrenaline surging at the unexpected interruption. She gripped the edge of her desk to center herself and looked up at Curtis, looming above her desk, his broad shoulders shifting impatiently.

"Ready for what?" She blinked a few times, her eyes dry from staring at the computer monitor too long. Deciphering the scratches and scrawls Curtis considered handwriting into flow charts and slide presentations took miracles. Hard work, experience, computer knowledge and miracles. If she got the slightest bit of it wrong, she'd likely have to start the entire presentation over. Which was why she had engrossed herself in the project completely, not allowing any outside distractions until his voice tickled at her ear.

How did he do that? Manipulate sound waves to feel like a touch?

"Dinner. I called to push back the reservation once. I could do it again if you need, but I haven't eaten since lunch." He gave her a smile that could make a leopard change its spots.

Focus, Heather. He's just smiling. Being friendly. "Do I need to drive you and—"

"No. He left when you were at lunch. The riverboats are a go. I've been working on the mall projects while you've been in the zone out here."

He stepped closer, leaning over her for a better look at her computer. The scent of his warm skin ignited her imagination. She swallowed hard, trying to block the image of him leaning just a little closer, swiping the piles of paper on her desk to the floor, and his strong, masculine hands lifting her from her chair and placing her on the cool mahogany.

"The Chicago high-rise. Pass what you've done to the New York office. I assigned the venture to a project manager this morning."

So much for fantasies. "I'll package up my notes and get everything ready to go out in the morning Fed Ex." She turned in her seat, stuffing papers back into their folders.

Curtis's warm hand drifted down on top of hers, covering it completely. Breath stuttered in her throat as she raised her gaze to his.

Just like this morning she was caught up in it, locked inside her own desire to do nothing but stare at him. Well, not nothing. But she didn't dare do enough to get herself fired.

"Let's get out of the office where we can talk." The husky inflection of his voice promised more than talking, more than dinner. And yet his eyes showed nothing at all. Only the intense blue-green stare.

Was he propositioning her? She had no idea how office romances started, but she didn't think men like Curtis Frye settled for women like her when they were accustomed to waif-thin models and collagen-injected starlets.

His lips tilted in a smile. "Are you ready?"

For what? With a nod of her head that did nothing to center her universe, currently spinning in all sorts of directions, she collected her purse and stood, finding herself in the same position that had struck her dumb this morning.

Fantasy and reality were morphing into one, turning the centimeters that separated their bodies into riots of electricity.

Okay, Heather. This is your last chance. If you don't want to give in and have an affair with your boss, leave right now. Because if he makes the slightest move, you know you'll be all over him.

"I'm ready."

"Great." With his hand protectively on the small of her back, he walked her out the outer door of his office and through the nearly empty floor. "Do you mind if I drive?"

Once inside the elevator she handed him the keys.

"After tonight the truck is all yours, I promise. No more having to drive me around."

"Except you're the one driving."

"True." He handed the keys back. "You should drive so you're used to it when you drop me off."

Drop him off? Laughter bubbled inside, but she tamped it down. Of course Curtis Frye wasn't asking her to dinner, he was asking her to drive him to dinner because he didn't have a car.

She fell in step beside him, nearly running into him when he stopped at the door to the parking garage.

"I should drive."

"It is hard to be your chauffeur when you never let me drive." She tried for a smile, but by his puzzled expression she must have missed.

"You're not my chauffeur. There might be photographers and it takes some aggressive driving to get around them. It can be frightening to try and maneuver a vehicle that size with people all around you."

Tilting her head, she pulled her purse higher on her

shoulder. “Do you want me to drive around front and pick you up?”

He stiffened, nostrils flaring. “No. That’s ridiculous.” He took the keys from her hand and opened the door. His head turned from side to side, then back to her. “There are two by the exit ramp. If we run, we can be inside before they get their cameras up.”

He didn’t wait for her assent, just grabbed her hand and pulled her across the nearly empty parking garage. He unlocked the doors with the remote, but it caused the headlights to flash, and the photographers to come running.

Breathless, Heather climbed up into her seat and slammed the door behind her. Before she got her seatbelt on, Curtis had started the engine and was pulling away. He nearly missed a photographer who tried to shove his lens against the tinted windows.

“Where did you make reservations for again?”

She listed the restaurants from memory. As Curtis maneuvered through the streets she realized he still had dinner plans. A ping of jealousy wiggled through her and she pushed her watch higher on her wrist.

“So, am I some kind of decoy for whomever you are meeting tonight?” The vinegar in her voice surprised her. Man, if she was going to be bitter about every woman he dated she *really* needed to find a different job. She’d go crazy if she had to get dinner reservations, arrange romantic getaways, buy gifts for the other woman.

She pressed her lips together in disgust. She was acting like a jealous wife, and she was his assistant, nothing more. But her attraction to him grew exponentially every day. It might not be safe for her sanity to stay much longer.

“We’re going to dinner so you and I can talk. I have a

brilliant idea, and I want you to keep an open mind when I tell you about it. But not while I'm trying to lose whomever is tailing us."

They drove in silence, Curtis pulling down a side street next to one of the restaurants she'd made reservations at, watching a blue sedan pull into the parking lot then speed away.

It didn't add up. He'd never run his ideas by her before. She noticed he didn't present them to anyone before he was sure of their response in his favor. Why would he need her opinion?

She rubbed the base of her neck where a headache was forming from having her thick hair pulled back so tightly for so long. She undid the clip and massaged the aching muscles with her fingers. Why couldn't anything about this day make sense?

Her world was waffling between fantasy and reality, and at the moment she wanted a little more fantasy in the mix. Like if she really was going to have dinner with Curtis, she wanted to look more like someone who'd be sharing a meal with him and less like, well, like his secretary. Ugh.

What she wouldn't give for a poof from a fairy godmother that could magically reduce the size of her hips and put her in a sexy red cocktail dress.

He pulled the SUV alongside the curb in front of the nondescript restaurant, housed in what used to be a warehouse. The best restaurants in San Francisco had nominal storefronts, and focused entirely on the food.

As Curtis rounded the front of the SUV and pulled open her door, she noticed a car speeding down the quiet street. A blinding flash and blaring headlights kept her from seeing much as Curtis pulled her against him.

"Let's get inside, quickly." He folded her hand in his and

urged her across the sidewalk and into the restaurant. The sound of tires spinning, then squealing, kept her nerves on high.

She knew Curtis dealt with the paparazzi, but never before had she experienced the terror firsthand. Her mind knew it was only a man with a camera, and yet her body reacted to the stranger, flashing lights, and the realization that her anonymity had been torn from her for a moment. She trembled after one run-in. How must Curtis feel to have been permanently skinned of his privacy?

"Are you all right?" He rubbed his hands up and down her arms, calming the raging emotions. "I'm sorry about that. I really thought I had lost him."

"It was a different car." Her pulse jackhammered, thundering in her ears. She forced herself to breathe slower, deeper.

"What?"

"The one we lost was blue. That one was silver."

He gave her a gentle squeeze on the shoulder. "Let's not let it ruin our evening."

"But why would they do something like that? Kendra has press releases with photos, and you have interviews all day on Friday. Isn't that enough?"

"Not for some of them." The apology in his tone made her heart sink. This was his life, every day.

She was thankful for the arrival of a dark-haired man who told Curtis everything had been set up according to his specifications, and asked them to follow him.

They passed through a darkened archway, into an empty dining room. Every table in the restaurant was covered in creamy cotton, with blue votive candles and snowball-like hydrangeas.

"I hope everything meets your needs, Mr. Frye."

"It's perfect." Curtis pulled out a chair at a table in the middle of the room, and, not quite sure what was happening, Heather sat.

The dark-haired man scurried past them, through a door leading to what she guessed was the kitchen. The room must be light and airy during the day, minimalist and fresh. But at night, with the lights turned down, candlelight flickering on the bare walls, bursts of blue hydrangeas everywhere, it was a summertime romance heaven. If this were a date. Which it seemed to be. Almost.

He hadn't asked her properly, or even asked her at all, really.

"You look nervous. Are you still upset about earlier?"

Which earlier did he mean? Arriving at her apartment before the morning paper? Not speaking to her once they were in the office, using email instead? The mad dash to the SUV, the paparazzi when they arrived at the restaurant?

"I think I have whiplash."

His gaze narrowed with worry. "I didn't realize you'd hurt yourself. Do you need to see a doctor?"

She shook her head. "Not from being blinded by flashbulbs. From this day. I'm not sure what is going on."

"If you're not sure, then I am doing something wrong."

"No, it's just—"

The man returned with a bottle of champagne and showed the label to Curtis. Probably real champagne from France, not the sparkling California wine most people passed off as champagne.

She reached up and ran her fingers through her hair,

wondering if she did indeed hit her head today. Maybe she bumped it in the shower this morning and everything since was simply a hallucination. Except she'd worked very hard today—and if she dreamed about work, she was truly pathetic.

Still, this wasn't her life. She didn't dine at five-star establishments; she ate at chain restaurants with massive margarita menus. Guys she dated didn't make reservations, let alone close down entire dining rooms for a private party. And she didn't drink real champagne. Not even once.

Curtis poured the champagne, the tiniest of bubbles bursting at the surface of the pale gold liquid. Champagne, a romantic restaurant, a day of feeling completely off-kilter. She was standing on the precipice and so much as a wink from him would push her over the edge.

She took the glass from his outstretched hand and tried to firm her footing. "Is this a date?"

His lips tilted in a smile. "Dating is for people who don't know each other. We know one another quite well, don't you think?"

She nodded in agreement, still perplexed. She knew him on paper, and in fantasies. Reality was another matter entirely. One he seemed to have no desire to help her out with.

She lifted her glass. "To the riverboat deal."

"To gambling on a sure thing." He clinked her glass and sipped his champagne, staring at her with hooded eyes.

Crisp sweetness flooded her mouth as she sipped, then the bubbles burst, tickling her mouth with the dry flavor of the grape. She loved it—real champagne was light years beyond the stuff they sold at the supermarket—but she wished it were vodka. Something strong to take the edge off her insecurities and fears. Curtis Frye was flirting with her, had done all this probably with sleeping with her in mind, which would be a fantastic idea if she could only get her conscience to quiet down.

He's your boss.

You won't be able to work with him after.

You'll have nothing but a memory when you leave.

A regret.

And yet she'd regret it either way. After tonight she'd always be uncomfortable working with him, whether she indulged herself in what he offered or not.

"More champagne?"

"Goodness, yes." She set her glass in front of him and stared as if he'd sprouted another head.

"Are you still upset about earlier?"

"I'm not upset, just confused." She lifted her now-full champagne flute and stared at the bubbles. "I'm not sure why we're here, what it is you want to talk about, and why you needed to clear an entire restaurant to do it."

"I wanted to make sure you know how much I appreciate all you do for me."

"You said that with the SUV. Which I think is mine, although I haven't actually driven it yet."

She had a grin that ignited his imagination. She wasn't the obvious beauty he was accustomed to, the overt brand of sexiness so common in the women he'd dated in the last few years. When he'd thought up his plan for her, he hadn't considered her a romantic possibility, hadn't considered the inclination until he'd seen the picture of her as a girl with Cinderella aspirations, and realized she held them still. She wanted romance. And romance could be bought.

Though as she stared at him, he realized the price was

much higher than he'd bargained for. She was a stunning combination of effortless, radiant sensuality with gentle, unaffected innocence.

That she had no idea what he had planned was written all over her face. And damn if she didn't look cute, trying not to be perplexed. She'd been like that her first few weeks on the job, never asking what he meant, just trudging forwards and finding things out for herself.

Her determination and loyalty made her the obvious choice for this action, but sitting alone with her in a now-private restaurant, he had to wonder if a part of him hadn't registered how green her eyes were, how fantastic she could look after an afternoon with his mother's expertise on appearance. It would truly be like Cinderella, polishing the pearl within.

All through dinner she studied him, and he could see the ebb and flow of brightness in her eyes as she followed through one hypothesis after another in her mind. It occurred to him she might think he was propositioning her for a simple office affair, and it bothered him a little that she seemed to be considering it. But then, sharing more than a workday with Heather Tindall held a new appeal.

"This day has been amazing." She twirled her spoon in the crème brulée. "But I must say dinner was even better."

"I'm glad you enjoyed it."

She set down her spoon and leaned back in her chair. "I've never had lavender in dessert before. I'll have to tell Stacia."

"The sleepy roommate?"

"The one with a boyfriend. She'll never believe this day." Heather's words flowed like a waterfall after the second glass of champagne. Since her third she'd been completely relaxed. "She'll think I dreamed everything."

"Why?"

"Please. I was bum-rushed by paparazzi, had dinner with California's most eligible bachelor, and he closed down one of the best restaurants in the city to talk to me about...wait. What was it you needed my opinion on?" She pushed her glasses tighter against her face, making him want to pull them off. The glasses had to go. She had the prettiest green eyes, a bright green that shouldn't be shrunken behind corrective lenses.

"I want you to know how much I appreciate all you've done for me."

Her brows knit together. "The raise and the car said that. Dinner wasn't necessary. Nice, but—"

"We work very well together. I'd like for us to do more of that."

"Are you promoting me?"

"Absolutely." He reached into his pocket, gripping the blue box in his fist. He shouldn't be nervous. This was business.

"But I'm not qualified to be a project manager." She shifted in her seat, her lips twisting.

"I was thinking of another position." He set the ring box on the table between them and opened it to face her.

"Glory be to Christmas trees, what is that?"

"An engagement ring."

Her mouth moved, no words coming out, as expressions raced across her face. Surprise, elation, distrust, anger, hope.

She reached out and shut the ring box with a snap. "It is time for me to wake up from this dream." She stood up, grabbing her purse from the floor.

"Heather, wait." He snatched up the ring box and followed her as she nearly ran out of the dining room, grabbing her just before she made it out the door and spinning her to face him.

A riot of color swirled on her face. The intense green of her glassy eyes, hot pink on her cheeks, a deeper rouge on her full lips, the rich brown of her hair spilling over her shoulders.

"I don't know what game you're playing, but I'm out." She spat the words like bullets.

"I'm not playing you. I want to be completely honest in what I expect."

Her mouth twisted wryly. "This whole day has been about playing me. It's cruel, Curtis. You can't put someone's emotions in a blender like this and then...then..."

"I need you."

"You do?" She flushed slightly, biting her lip.

He nodded slowly. "I know it's not the fairy tale you want, but I need you."

"You need me to make your office run smoothly, not to be your wife."

"It's not what you think."

"I have no idea *what* to think."

"The paparazzi tonight explained it in ways words never could. Until they see me as settled in a relationship, they'll take every dinner, every outing where a woman is involved, as a possible social affair instead of judging me on the merits of my actions. If the world thinks we're engaged, life would be considerably easier for me. But it wouldn't be just for me. You'll have everything you've ever dreamed of. I'm in a position to take care of you completely."

"I don't want your money."

"That's one of the reasons why I want *you*."

I want you. The words hung in the air between them. Heather's eyes fluttered closed and he knew he was almost there.

"It won't be forever. A year at the high end, and you'll be

free to live your life with security enough to do as you please. Start a business, travel, go back to school. I can give you what you need, anything you've ever dreamed of."

"I know," she whispered, leaning forward until her forehead rested on his shoulder.

Chapter Four

Exhausted didn't begin to cover it. Sliding the bags through the front door, Curtis stepped through and then closed it behind him as quietly as he could. After a week of criss-crossing the country, trying to salvage the over-budget tram project in Portland and the stalled Chicago high-rise, the last thing he needed upon coming home was to wake up Mrs. Rutledge.

He loved her, but she'd left messages saying they needed to have a chat once he got home, and he didn't care to. She was either going to retire or grill him about the engagement announcement, and he didn't want to deal with either scenario until he had a full night's sleep.

"Are you hungry?"

He jumped at the sound of the voice behind him. Of course she would have waited up. She worried about him beyond comprehension, which was why she'd elected herself his housekeeper long before he could afford one.

"I'll make you a sandwich. Come into the kitchen."

With a grin on his face, he shook his head and followed her into the kitchen, flicking on the light. The Mexican tile and hanging copper pots gave the room a warm feel, the bright colors livening the space. The decorator had balked when he instructed her to let Mrs. Rutledge choose everything. Now he was glad he hadn't resorted to the granite and stainless steel that twit had suggested.

Curtis tugged the knot of his tie until it loosened. "I can make my own sandwich. You should get some rest."

"Don't be silly." She bustled about the room in her lavender robe, gathering what he would need. From the refrigerator she pulled out a turkey sandwich, already cut on the diagonal and garnished with a bunch of grapes.

"I see you've baited the trap. If I'm about to be lectured, that requires cake." He undid the buttons of his suit jacket and shrugged it off, draping it across a barstool.

With a huff of exasperated breath she procured a slice of cheesecake. His eyes widened. That did not bode well. He'd never had a lecture that required cheesecake before. Lemon or chocolate, sure, but cheesecake?

"Are you retiring?" He turned away so he wouldn't have to watch her answer, taking a glass from the cupboard and filling it with water.

"No, why? Does Heather want to run the house herself?"

"Heather?" He sat at a barstool, pulling the sandwich to him.

"Your fiancée. Heather Tindall. That sweet girl who's been pining after you for months. You never even gave her any notice, then you turn up with her at your parents' house and announce your engagement, only to disappear the next day." Her lips compressed into a tight line and her arms folded across her chest.

He tunneled his fingers through his hair, wondering if he could trust her with the truth. Probably, but she wouldn't approve of that either.

"Jason, this is not a good idea."

"You like her. You never like anyone I'm seeing." He bit into the sandwich, trying not to think how different this reaction was from his parents'. They'd been wide-eyed and caught off guard, but the idea of a wedding in the future was enough to keep his mother at bay. His father had declared Heather perfect marriage material, but warned him not to let his personal life encroach on work.

"Do you like her, or are you taking advantage of the poor thing?"

"Poor thing? Heather can take care of herself." Wasn't she supposed to be worried Heather might be taking advantage of him?

"Not where you are concerned. Jason, you don't hear the way she talks about you."

"She's not starry-eyed, she knows exactly who I am." His heart stalled as their eyes met. Heather might know everything there was to know about Curtis Frye, but he'd never mentioned Jason Curtis. Junior or Senior. Damn.

Had she agreed because of the power and prestige he now wielded? Would she be like the other women he'd dated, finding the first excuse to end things as soon as they learned he wasn't truly a Frye, but the son of a man in prison for murder? If she had, telling her could ruin everything.

"That is not what I am worried about." Unfolding her arms, she linked her hands together in front of her robe. "I don't understand what prompted this. The two of you weren't dating."

"I'll admit, it was a fast decision. But we know each other very well, and you know I've always thought very highly of her."

Irritation flashed in her gray eyes. "Don't start lying to me now, Jason. We've always been honest with each other."

"If you'll calm down for a minute, I'll explain."

Mrs. Rutledge stuffed her hands into the pockets of her robe. "I don't think I am going to like what you have to say."

He rolled his eyes. "It's a convenient publicity arrangement."

She lowered her head, shaking it slowly.

"Heather agreed. She'll be compensated generously."

She glanced up, her eyes looking as if they could pierce shards of ice into him. "There isn't enough money in the world to mend a broken heart, Jason."

The image of Heather crying in his office flashed in his mind. "I won't hurt her. That's not what this is about. I'm tired of not being seen for my accomplishments. Everything I do is tinged with some playboy rumor and I want to be taken seriously."

"What does that have to do with a nice girl like Heather?"

"I trust Heather. Would you rather I chose some parasite with no intention of holding up her end of the bargain?"

"I'd rather you chose someone you loved, instead of someone who loves you and will be heartbroken when you end the game."

"She is not in love with me. Wealth is a powerful aphrodisiac. Once she has her own money, she won't care what happens to me." Tension edged into his shoulders at the thought.

"Who are you trying to fool here, Jason? This scheme of yours will not work without someone getting hurt, and I don't want to see that happen to either of you. Why risk it?"

It hadn't felt like a risk. An emotion he didn't recognize niggled at the center of his chest. He frowned, his enthusiasm deflated. "I promise, I won't hurt her."

"You proposed and left town, leaving her to deal with your

mother, alone. I've been running interference, but the woman wants a wedding date. The least you could do is make up a story about wanting to take Heather to an island somewhere and elope."

Curtis blinked. "You already knew it was a front, didn't you?" He grabbed for the cheesecake. He'd earned it.

Mrs. Rutledge chuffed, shaking her head. "It's a front all right, but not for what you think."

His mouth full of cheesecake, he couldn't ask what she meant before she'd turned and left the kitchen.

"Soon, Mom. You'll meet him soon." Heather nestled the phone between her neck and shoulder, shuffling the photos on her desk.

"Baby, when your sisters got engaged they—"

"Mom, they were both younger than me when they got married, *and* living at home. Besides, Curtis isn't the ask-permission type." And it wasn't that kind of engagement. For Curtis it was business, but in time she might bring him around to see things her way.

If she hadn't agreed to his scheme, his determination might have sent him fiancée-shopping, and seeing him with another woman who might take advantage of the situation did not sit right. She'd made him consider her by working hard and being indispensable to him. Now, she had better access to show him how things could be if he let himself feel something for her. It was the only hope she had to be more to him than an employee. He'd love her. Someday.

"How did things go with his parents?"

"Good, I think. His mom wants to help choose the gown, and she had some advice for how I should dress after the wedding."

"She told you what to wear?"

In the most fluidly manipulative way possible, without a hint of rudeness. "Curtis says she does it for everyone in the family. She likes them to look a certain way."

"I repeat, she told you what to wear? And he let her?"

She couldn't help but laugh. "At the time it seemed helpful."

"Is he a mama's boy?"

"No, Mom." Not even close. His housekeeper seemed to know him better than his parents. The family was polite and cordial, but not hang-out-in-your-pajamas casual like hers. There was a lot of love there, but it was consolidated, coordinated to match the situation. "It's not like that. He feels very grateful to them, so he tries to go along with what they want."

"Why?"

Heather shifted in her seat. "He was adopted."

"So?"

His other siblings weren't. Of course, since she and her sisters were adopted, her mother wouldn't appreciate that Curtis saw a difference between biological and adopted children. And she agreed—so she couldn't even try and argue his side.

"Having his mother select a designer wardrobe for me isn't really something to get upset about."

"Hold on, honey. His mother is buying your clothes?" Her own mother's fingernails clicked in the background.

"It's fine, Mom. His sisters have gorgeous clothes. I'd love to have their hand-me-downs." Heck, she'd love to fit in their hand-me-downs. She stifled the sigh. She hadn't had a blended coffee since Curtis's proposition. "He said the talk of clothes was a sign of acceptance." Best to leave out the part where she'd been scheduled at the family hairdresser and make-up artist for wedding consultations.

"So his mother still dresses her children? Good gracious, you all refused to shop with me once you were out of elementary school."

"She's very good at it. She was a designer before she had kids."

"Please be careful. You don't have to change anything to make them like you. Curtis loves you because of who you are."

If only. "I'm fine, Mom." She plucked the property listing for the private island in the middle of Lake Shastina from the top of the pile of papers. "I called about Sapphire Isle."

"For the wedding? Getting everyone there would be a logistics nightmare. They only have the one dock."

If only there were an actual wedding to plan. "Golden is looking for existing resort properties."

"It's a private estate, Heather. The island is only three square miles. I doubt that would be of interest to a corporation as large as Golden City. They want huge lots of land."

"Actually, they want privacy. Sapphire Isle has that. Is the listing on your website current?" Curtis kept vetoing proposals from the rest of the staff, but by typing up all his rejections, she thought she had a lead on what he did want.

"Yes, nothing has changed. We show it a few times a year, rent it out even less."

"When can we see it?"

"Sapphire Isle? Are you looking for someplace to

honeymoon? You really should try something more exotic."

Honeymoon. Only if she got really lucky. Bringing Curtis around was going to be a slow process. Especially since she'd seen him twice in the last month, and one of those times was to sign his beloved contract. New Orleans needed his attention more than his quasi-relationship, chiefly because his PR guru was creating it. She smiled, remembering how he'd said he trusted her to handle the publicity, but there was no one to trust with his projects in Louisiana. It had come with a kiss. On the forehead, but still.

"Curtis wants privacy, and with the flight restrictions over Lake Shastina since it is at the base of Mount Shasta, Sapphire Isle is perfect." Not to mention she might be able to coax him into letting her work on the project with him. Transforming the estate into a private resort fit his plans. And since her parents had held the listing for so long, Heather had dreamed of ways to re-do it for years. Getting her ideas on paper should speed up the process and leave them time to figure things out. In bed. If at all possible.

"I'll fax over the rental agreement this afternoon." Papers rustled in the background.

"No, Mom. Curtis wants to buy Sapphire Isle."

Banging and bumping clanged in her ear. She pulled the phone away and smiled.

"Sorry. I dropped the phone. I thought you said Curtis wants to buy Sapphire Isle." The property her parents had been trying to sell for the better part of a decade.

"If he agrees, we'll need to rush escrow." The scream on the other end of the line made her laugh out loud. She listened to her mother yell the sale across the office.

The phone clicked in her ear. "Not so fast, babe." Her father's voice came across the line. "When do we get to meet this boy?"

✧

"So, what do you think?" Her green eyes sparkled with excitement, her fingertips tapping the edge of his desk.

Curtis blinked, forcing his gaze back to the file she'd presented him with. He'd been doing that all day, looking at her instead of concentrating on work. It was a good thing he was only in town for two days. Ever since she'd agreed to the relationship charade he'd been preoccupied with what she did, how she moved.

After his conversation with Mrs. Rutledge, he couldn't forget her warnings that Heather was in love with him. That alone should be reason enough for him to call off the ploy, but instead it made him study her even closer. He couldn't afford this kind of distraction permanently.

"I think it fits what you are looking for," Heather began, twisting her hands in front of her. Good thing the desk was between them. If not, he might reach out and calm the movement. "The privacy and exclusivity of a deluxe resort with the comfort and intimacy of a bed-and-breakfast. The perfect compromise for someone with too much money who wants to be catered to and left alone."

His lips curved as he raised an eyebrow. "Too much money?"

"It's not what you wanted, is it?" Her expression faltered and she lifted her glasses closer to her face. "I'm sorry. I know you're swamped. I shouldn't have wasted your time."

"The inspection reports are here as well?" He thumbed through the file. The estate fit his concept in every way but one—it sat in the middle of Lake Shastina in Northern

California. He'd been thinking tropical.

"Yes. Everything that needs fixing on the house is cosmetic. When the board objected to the project, you said you'd put up your own money for the first one, so I didn't want any surprises. My parents have had the listing for years. There is nothing wrong with the property."

"Then why has it been listed for years?"

"Location."

"I'm afraid that is the same problem we have now."

"No." Heather shook her head, a wisp of brown hair falling forward. "To live in, it's too remote, but not for a vacation, an escape. You don't want to live in the middle of nowhere, but visiting is fantastic for recharging your batteries."

He nodded and looked at the report she'd drafted again. She had a point, and there were certain security aspects of a private island that gave the property even more potential. But then everything seemed to hold promise when Heather presented it. Like the way she stepped to the side of his desk, leaning closer to see the folder and giving him a close-up shot of her feminine curves where the vee of her blouse dipped.

Curtis hooked a finger in the collar of his shirt and tugged. He had no idea what to do with this developing attraction to Heather, so he stuck to business. "It's worth the risk. Go ahead and put the deal in motion."

She clapped her hands like a child at the circus, then set one on his shoulder and squeezed. The heat of her fingers seared down his arm, curling his fingers. His whole body began to teeter on the knife's edge of desire. He could probably have her here, now, but he'd never taken a woman before he knew a way out of the scenario. But then, he'd never wanted one this bad, beyond his common sense.

"You won't be sorry, I promise." She removed her hand,

smoothing it against her skirt.

“I know.” He rolled his shoulders, trying to rid himself of the imprint she’d left, but it only served to spread the heady feeling across his chest, and lower. “I’d like for you to work up some redesign ideas so we can begin the remodel as soon as we clear escrow.”

“Me?” She backed her way to the far side of his desk. “I think a project manager would be better suited—”

“Normally, that would be the path, but since I am funding it myself I’d need to do the legwork. Right now I don’t have time.”

“But I don’t know what I am doing. I’ve never managed a project before, let alone one on a multi-million-dollar estate!”

“I trust you.” With more than she could ever know. “I’ll be sure to check your ideas before any decisions are made. Consider it hands-on training. You might want to run your own business some day. Managing a project can give you some insight into that.”

She nodded, twisting her hands again. No, not her hands this time, the ring. The one he’d given her.

“Do you need to have it sized?” He tilted his chin towards the symbol of their bond.

“What? Oh, the ring. No. It’s a nervous habit, I guess.” She hid her hands behind her back.

“Are you having second thoughts?” His stomach clenched at the idea.

She heaved a heavy sigh. “Your mother is trying to have me fitted for a wedding dress, and Kendra is trying to set up interviews and photo shoots. She says people are beginning to ask questions, and if I don’t do my part, our being together will make the paparazzi worse instead of better.”

He lifted a brow, "Do you think she suspects anything?"

"Kendra? No, she's just great at getting people to do what she wants."

Curtis squared his shoulders and closed the folder. "Here's what we do. I'll tell them both we are planning to elope privately without a lavish ceremony. That should put my mother's attentions on me, trying to convince me to let her have a wedding."

"Let *her* have a wedding?" Heather laughed at him. Laughed. She didn't know his mother very well.

"As for Kendra, I think the less press you do, the better." Her face fell and he knew he'd given the wrong answer. "Unless there is something you *want* to do."

Her cheeks lifted in a smile. "A photo shoot sounds like fun. I've never done one."

"If you want to, but keep Kendra with you for interviews." He didn't need some over-eager reporter twisting her words.

Heather practically shone as she left his office. Curtis closed his eyes, wondering how his simple plan had become so complicated.

Chapter Five

"Are you sure you want to do this?" Kendra's voice on the phone grated on Curtis's nerves. She'd asked him the same question every day for the last two months.

"Very." Each day he grew more certain this would be the best business decision he'd ever made. Already he could see the difference in the press. The only time his name was in bold, it referred to his work, or Heather's interest in bridal regalia.

"Did you get my email?"

"Which one?" Sitting at the small table in his hotel suite, he scrolled through the messages in his inbox. Heather condensed everything into one message—from his itinerary to transaction details she was ironing out. Kendra seemed to shoot him an email whenever a random idea popped into her head.

"The *Stylish* article—the one with the engagement details and pictures of Luxe."

"Saw it. Liked it. Is that all?" With one hand he loosened his tie, glancing at the alarm clock that reminded him he only had five hours until his next flight.

"And when have you scheduled the photo shoot?"

How he hated to have his picture taken. "Ask Heather."

"Your fiancée claims there is no time. I suggest the two of you figure it out. The only shots of you together are candids. I'm tempted to doctor something up before the tabloids take it as a sign this whole charade is manufactured."

He stiffened, his pulse hammering in his ears. "Excuse me?"

"You usually date very publicly, Curtis. This is a hard sell."

"I'm not selling anything. This is a real relationship, not something you've contrived for publicity. I'm living my life, doing my job. If it's not newsworthy, all the better."

"I'm trying to keep this as low-key as I can, but California's most eligible bachelor marrying his secretary is news. It's a Cinderella story, and magazines love that kind of spin."

He couldn't hold in his laugh. Cinderella had gotten them all in this game in the first place.

"What's so funny?"

"Have you run that Cinderella theory by Heather? She'd love it."

"Good to know. It's the theme of the photo spread *Bridal Party* wants to do with her."

"Don't twist her arm on any of this, Kendra. If she says no, you back off."

"Are you kidding? She's a bridal tour de force. She and your mother went to the bridal show this week and were photographed—"

"Don't tell me. Whatever she wants is fine by me." His mother had really taken Heather on as her protégée, even roping her into helping with charity events. It was a little too cozy for his liking, but it did lend authenticity as well as throw the scent off him.

Kendra didn't bother to hide her sigh. "Are you really sure you want to do this?"

"Heather is fantastic. End of discussion."

"Not that. Are you sure you want to do this to her? She loves you, Curtis. She's not like the other women you've dated who understood the game."

"Heather knows what she's getting into."

She hadn't balked at the confidentiality agreement, hadn't haggled the terms of any of the contracts she signed. Well, except to ask if there was a fidelity clause. Which there was. He had no intention of embarrassing her publicly, or allowing himself to be embarrassed.

Kendra cleared her throat. "Are you actually planning on marrying her? Your attention span with women has never been that long. I like her, and so I'm saying I don't think she has any idea what she's really signed on for."

"Everyone likes Heather. Me most of all. Don't worry. I'd never do anything to hurt her."

When he clicked off the line and turned off the phone, he stared at it for a minute. Soon this part of his life would be over, Heather's influence creating enough of a shadow for him to evade the world of society pages and gossip columns.

He needed this relationship for his sanity, but he wasn't selfish enough to get that at the expense of Heather's feelings. He would not hurt her. She'd have everything she ever wanted. He'd make sure of it.

Heather winced at the bright lights stinging her eyes and heating the church to a deplorable degree. The old stone building had no air conditioning, as if she needed another reason to sweat besides half her family tagging along to watch the photo shoot. That's what she got for suggesting they set the Cinderella-themed piece in her hometown.

"A little more emotion, Heather," the photographer called out, clicking his shutter. "You have to give me something." He turned to Kendra. "Make her lose the glasses and stop acting frigid."

Frigid? She was practically melting. Her throat ached and tears stung at her eyes, but she didn't dare let them fall. No telling how long they'd have her in the makeup chair again.

Kendra swished over to her, flicking her sheet of black hair off her shoulder with her long, manicured nails. "Listen, honey, I know you aren't used to this, but you have to try."

"I am trying." She clutched at the pink tulle of the bridal gown she wore, wishing she could take a deep breath. No dice, they'd laced her so tight into the corset she couldn't even sit down. "The other photographers haven't been so demanding."

"Those were candid shoots, Heather. You just had to be yourself and have a bridal shower or pick out the dress with Curtis's mother. This is a formal photograph with the possibility of making the cover if you could just relax."

"I don't know what I am supposed to do."

"Pretend it is your wedding day." She must have pulled a face because Kendra's eyes widened in alarm. "Or don't. I know you two don't want any of this hoopla, but we need these photos for the magazine. If you keep looking awkward and tense, the reporter we did the interview with this morning will put that in her piece. Is that what you want?"

"You know it isn't."

"Then smile, and do as he asked and lose the glasses." Kendra swiped for them, but Heather batted her hand away.

"Without them, I can't see a thing."

"That might help," Curtis surprised them both by saying from behind the photographer. He stood with his arms folded across his broad chest, his feet spread apart to make him appear even larger.

Good night, if he were a picture in a catalog, she'd be ordering overnight delivery. Heather's cheeks tightened in a smile as his gaze met hers.

"I thought you wouldn't be in until tonight?" she asked, releasing her dress and trying to stand up tall. She was supposed to have time for her father to pick her up from the church and run home and change before he arrived so they could survey the Sapphire Island property together.

He tilted his head towards Kendra and gave her a knowing smile as he stepped over the power cords littering the floor. As he made his way to her with confident strides, her toes curled in her too-tight heels. When he raised a hand to her face she thought he might touch her, but instead he lifted the frames off her face and stepped back.

"I can't see a thing." She reached out a hand, catching him about the wrist to steady herself. Her heart raced, and she told herself it was the fear of being blind to anyone farther away than he was. Not because his presence sped up her pulse.

"We're getting your vision corrected. Don't you have contacts?"

"I hate them," she said through clenched teeth. There was no way she could wear both contacts and eye make-up. Both felt like grit in her eyes and together they were a lethal combination. Her mother had selected a new brand for her and presented them as a bridal-shower gift last night, but she hadn't wanted to risk trying them today.

"Yes!" exclaimed the photographer. "Very pouty. I like it."

Releasing Curtis, she turned towards the shutterbug. "I am not pouting."

"Frye, touch her again. With you here we seem to be getting

some emotion out of her. I'll frame it so you're out of the picture. From the waist up she doesn't look so heavy."

A few more clicks and Heather was so mad she could have spit glass at the man. Not to mention Curtis, who began to stroke her hand as if Mr. Snaps-a-lot hadn't just called her fat *and* frigid.

"How about a few of them together?" Kendra asked, a dastardly grin on her face.

So she'd known Curtis was coming. She could have issued a warning. Something so Heather wasn't so unprepared as Curtis sidled next to her on the steps of the church altar.

Jolly holly sticks, they were standing in front of church pews filled with people, she in full bridal regalia, and he in a dark suit. He took her hands and stared into her eyes. Heather had to squeeze her eyes tight, trying to steel herself against the waves of emotion hitting her from all sides. Here was all she ever wanted, and none of it was real.

"Closer," the photographer ordered. She held still, but Curtis moved to her, enveloping her in his arms.

Taking a deep breath, she opened her eyes and tilted her head up to look at him. "Did you change your cologne?"

His chest shook as he laughed silently. "Not wearing any."

"Perfect! More of that!"

Heather rolled her eyes at the photographer's instruction, melting deeper into Curtis as she whispered, "I hate him."

Curtis dipped his head, pressing his forehead onto hers. "He's just doing his job," he said through a smile, never once moving his lips.

"Insulting me is his job?" And isn't it yours to defend me?

"He was right. You need to relax or you'll hate the pictures." Curtis straightened, running a finger down her cheek. Her blood heated at his tender touch, her mind unsure if this was real or for the cameras.

The photographer stepped too close for her to reply without his overhearing. “How about a kiss?”

Curtis tilted his head, leaning closer. Her pulse stalled as her hand found the center of his chest and pushed. He was really about to have their first kiss photographed in front of a live audience. She stepped back, teetering as one of the shoes came off. The bumpy carpet soothed her foot, but did nothing for the ire rising inside.

“I don’t think so.” She narrowed her eyes at Curtis, squinting to see his reaction.

“I can’t believe this,” the photographer mumbled, slithering out of her focus.

“Heather, come here.” Curtis held out a hand. The dangerously appealing charm of it all unnerved her. “Let’s get this over with.”

Heather shook her head, realizing she couldn’t pretend any more. She’d agreed to play along in the hopes he would open his eyes and see her, the potential they had together. But even here he didn’t feel a thing, insisted on living life by going through the motions.

No one knew none of it was real. No one would ever know. Sure, everyone had been surprised by how quickly things happened, but never doubted the story she fed them. No one, not even her two sisters watching this whole charade, realized Curtis Frye thought of her only as his assistant. And always would.

Her mouth went as dry as the bottom of a birdcage, her heart pounding so fast against her ribs she knew it must be quaking the silk of her dress. At once she broke out in a sweat and felt chilled to the bone. What had she done?

She'd sold herself to him for a dream. Now that she'd awoken, she had to face a reality worse than any nightmare. As much as she adored him, it wouldn't be enough to make it right. None of this was right. Perfect, but not right.

How could she have done this to him? To her family? To herself? Make a mockery out of the one thing she'd ever truly wanted?

Everyone stared at her, watching and waiting for her to do something. She felt their collective urging, telling her to move. Beneath her diamond-crusted tiara her scalp tingled with the sweat of panic. Humiliation and heartbreak stung bitterly at her mouth. She couldn't do this now, or ever. She had no choice. She grabbed the train of her dress, squinted her eyes to make out the safest path, and ran.

So much for most eligible bachelor. The top fifty sexiest men list too. Though, if Curtis Frye had his choice, being left at the altar was not how he would have opted off both lists. Kendra had already made a joke about it, saying it best to be jilted at a photo shoot than in reality. She was trying to feed the two reporters a line about nerves and pressure, but from their eagerness to get on their cell phones it was obvious they didn't buy it.

Dear God, he had to get out of here, away from the media frenzy that would follow. He probably had another thirty minutes before helicopters arrived and the piranhas started swirling. He needed a fast, and foolproof, escape.

It came to him in a flash, the one place he could go for privacy, an island estate he'd bought, not a half hour's drive from here. He'd had his boat moved from the bay, and it was waiting at the dock. Once he crossed Lake Shastina and made his way to the island, no one could get to him before he was ready.

He needed a plan for how he would handle the fallout. Kendra would come up with a scheme of some kind, but more than likely it would shine a bad light on Heather. And as angry as he was with her, he didn't want for her to be humiliated.

It was enough that he was. All those eyes turning on him as Heather lifted her skirts and ran back down the stairs of the church. He'd chased her, almost caught her, until her father pulled up and whisked her away.

Hell, he'd even picked up the shoes she'd ditched to make her escape.

He leaned against the pillar at the side of the stairs, held up the shiny silver heels and shook his head. She'd had her chance to play Cinderella, to be her own fairy godmother. A happily ever after wasn't waiting around the corner—lawsuits and damage control were. Prince Charming might have chased the girl all over the kingdom, but Heather hadn't been standing next to a prince.

Which was probably why she ran. He wanted to find her, make sure she was all right, coax her into continuing the scheme. Instead, he decided to face that this was something that could never work. Curtis shook his head and started for his car. Heather would be fine. She could start over someplace else with complete anonymity.

He kept walking, knowing that finding Heather Tindall was the absolute last thing he needed to do.

Heather lay down on the small bed, her dress wilting around her. Really, she should have worn something underneath, or packed an appropriate suitcase rather than being stuck with the one her friends thought she might need, her friends who expected her to have a real honeymoon and a real wedding. But she hadn't planned on trying to escape reporters before she got out of the dress and into something with proper undergarments.

Why did they choose a dress that laced up the back?

Right up until that photographer started talking, and then Curtis remained forever frozen, the entire day had been a little girl's dream. And what did dreams get you?

Nightmares.

Curtis would fire her. Her sisters would laugh behind her back for the rest of her life. Curtis's PR guru would persecute her in the press. She might be completely unemployable. And there was a clause in the contract that allowed Curtis to sue her for such behavior. Not that he could get blood from a turnip, but the threat of permanent poverty should have kept her from running away. And yet, her heart had taken over.

Stupid fairy tale fantasies. She reached up, trying to free the veil and tiara from her head. Pins held her hair in an upswept cascade of curls, a style that had taken two hours to put in and promised to take twice as long to find all the pins holding everything in place.

If her hair wouldn't budge, she'd settle for losing the hoop skirts holding the layers of silk miles from her body. She stood, lifting the layers until she found what she hoped was the tie to the skirts. She'd put them on before the dress, then dove into the creation with the help of three people.

The skirts dropped in a whoosh, the air hitting her legs.

"Damn."

Heather tried to ignore the thumping of her heart as she hurriedly dropped her skirts and faced the man behind the voice she'd never forget.

"What are you doing here?" she squeaked.

The blue-green gaze cut at her beneath heavy-lidded eyes. "It's my boat."

"Right." She smoothed her hands down the skirt of the dress, the beading tickling her palms. "Right. I didn't think you'd come here today."

"I did have other plans, but they ended up here too."

"I know you're upset—"

"Upset would have been *Curtis, I can't go through with this* in private."

"I'm sorry." Her chin trembled and she clenched her jaw to rein in her emotions. She didn't get to be the one who cried right now. Not after the spectacle she'd made in public.

"I know you are." He set the suitcase he carried on the floor of the small cabin of the cruiser. "How are you?"

Heather sank back down onto the bed, staring at the hoop skirts pooling at her bare feet. "I've been better."

She raised her face to meet his cool blue gaze, no emotion showing through his polished façade. Maybe she shouldn't have put the contacts in once she'd cried her eye makeup off. Knowing it was one thing, but seeing it was another. At once she knew she'd love him forever, and running out was the smartest decision she'd ever make. She'd lost herself in him for a few months, let herself get wrapped up in the promise of perfect until she could barely see her way out.

She'd hoped indulging his fake-relationship scheme would help him see his way into the real thing, but he had no intention of ever opening himself up that way. She knew she felt things too intensely at times, but it was far better than feeling nothing at all.

"What are you doing here?" The husky purr to his voice tickled her ear, making her shiver.

"I thought I would hide."

"On my boat?" Laughter tinged his voice.

"No, on the island." She pulled her bottom lip between her teeth, trying not to think he looked even better now, out of the suit and in jeans and an oxford shirt the same color as his eyes. She'd never seen him this dressed down before.

"And how were you going to get there?"

"I was going to take the boat."

Curtis laughed, leaning his shoulder against the doorjamb. "You've never driven a boat, let alone one this size. You told me yourself. That's why we had to have someone ferry you to the house last week to tour the property with the inspector."

She squared her shoulders. "It can't be that hard. There has to be a manual somewhere."

Laughter erupted from him and he slumped down into the chair bolted by the door.

"What?"

"Frye's Runaway Bride Stranded in Lake Shastina. Story at eleven."

"Oh, stuff it. I'd have figured it out well enough."

"So what were you waiting for? Why haven't you made this great escape?"

She shifted, trying not to let his stare bother her. "I needed to change my clothes."

"So, change."

"I can't get out of the dress by myself."

"You should have thought about that before you had your dad drop you off here."

"I did. He should be back with my suitcase any minute now."

"And what is that?" He nodded towards the pink case sitting on the table beside the bed.

The blush heated her from the roots of her hair all the way down to her toes. *That* was the largest collection of lingerie she'd ever seen. And there was no way she could ask her father to help untie her dress, only to put on clothes she had no business wearing in the first place.

"Wedding presents."

"You don't get to keep the presents if you don't actually have a wedding, and we were never going to."

Yes, she'd read that loud and clear at the church. "Not from the wedding, from the bridal shower. One of the magazines wanted to photograph mine, so we held it yesterday."

"Well, you certainly look the part of bride, so I suppose you do get to keep them. But we have a problem bigger than wedding etiquette."

"Which one?"

"Right now there is the issue of you, on my boat, planning on going to my island, and I suppose stay at my house, though you have no desire to be with me."

"That's not it."

"Then what is it, Heather? What was so important you had to put on a performance like that? Are you trying to renegotiate for a better contract?"

"No!" Her hands balled into fists, her fingernails biting at her palms.

He blew out a breath. "Did someone put you up to this?"

"No!"

He looked her straight in the eye. "Then what?"

"I just can't pretend anymore." Her throat hardened as if her heart had lodged there.

He rolled his eyes. "Another half hour, so you could have told me without witnesses, would have killed you?"

"I'm not you! You think things out twice beforehand. I actually have emotions, react to situations. You go through life like a robot." Her voice took on a thick, strained quality.

"Of all the people to be juvenile and petty—"

"Me?" Her eyes widened and she blinked furiously to hold back the tears. "How mature is it to dream up a fake relationship to get out of the limelight? Glass houses, Curtis."

"Glass slippers, Heather." She hadn't noticed her shoes in his hand until he held them up, then pitched them at the opposite wall. "What kind of game are you playing?"

She closed her eyes, lowering her head in defeat. "I didn't take them off for you to come find me."

"And yet I did, find you, here on *my* boat."

She stood, lifting the skirts of her dress so she could walk. "I took them off because I couldn't run in heels that high. No other blooming reason." She stepped towards the door of the cabin, tripped on the hoopskirts at her feet and fell directly into Curtis's arms. He righted her, shifting from the doorway so she could leave.

"I am not your Prince Charming," he hissed into her ear. "And I never promised to be."

"Don't I know it," she mumbled, trudging up the stairs. On deck her heart thudded even harder than it had when Curtis stepped into the cabin. The parking lot of the marina was filled to bursting, photographers and lookey-loos everywhere.

She couldn't go out there, face them, and have them hound her while she waited like a teenager for her father to come pick her up.

As if none of them had ever seen a woman in a wedding gown on the deck of a yacht before, the crowd started humming in anticipation. A half dozen or so grabbed their cameras and made their way towards the boat.

"Holy schnikey," she whispered, her eyes heavy with tears. Panic flooded her mind, froze her feet to the spot. She could not push her way through them. They'd eat her alive.

"Deep breath, then smile."

Curtis's whisper behind her became the only sound she could make out above the pounding of her heartbeat, the rushing of adrenaline-soaked blood in her ears. "It's all going to be fine." He wrapped an arm around her waist and turned her to him, away from the onslaught rushing towards the boat. "Just relax."

"I can't." She hated to whine but her jaw felt so tense she could barely open her mouth. "I can't go out there and you want—"

He silenced her mouth and her mind with one brush of his lips against hers. Her senses came alive—the soft, firm feel of his lips against hers, the fresh peppermint taste of his mouth as her lips parted for him, the warm smell of his skin. In her mind's eye she saw them at the altar of the church, sharing this kiss she'd dreamed of for so long.

He pulled back, pressing his forehead to hers. "See? It's not so hard."

Her heart stalled. Did he mean kissing her, or lying?

Curtis pulled her tighter against him. "When I am done talking, you wave and smile, then get below deck." He spoke through his pasted-on grin, not waiting for her to respond. Reporters and town gossips had almost made it down the dock to the boat.

"Sorry about today, everybody." He spoke loud enough for even those still in the parking lot to hear. "Just a little case of cold feet. We're off to warm them up." He planted a kiss on her temple and gave her a gentle nudge towards the stairs as he released her. On autopilot, she waved, smiled and darted down the stairs, flopping onto the bed as the engines of the boat roared to life around her.

"You didn't change." After securing the yacht at the private dock, and calling to put the security team on alert, Curtis opened the door and went below deck, finding Heather lying on the bed, her hands pressed on her eyes. Too bad it wasn't like last time, when he'd stumbled upon her, skirts hitched up to her waist, sheer white panties—

"I can't get out of the dress by myself." At least that's what it sounded like she said.

"You want me to help you change before we go to the house?"

She sat straight up, her eyes so wide he feared they might roll out of her head. "What if they take pictures?"

"The paparazzi? They can't get in range with a helicopter because of the airspace restrictions, but telescopic lenses might work from shore. You told me that, remember? When you told me about the property?"

Heather nodded. With a sigh she turned to the pink case. "I don't have anything to change into."

"What in the world is in that suitcase?"

"Nothing I'll need." Heather stood, marching out of the cabin and up the stairs. Curtis grabbed her suitcase and his, following her on deck.

Setting the cases on the dock, he turned back to the boat

and lifted Heather over the rail. She squeaked and clung to him until he set her on her feet.

“What did you do that for?” She pressed against his chest, but he didn’t let go his hold on her waist. The dress was the softest silk he’d ever felt.

“I didn’t want you to trip on your dress like last time.”

“Last time I tripped on my hoop skirt, not my dress.” She tried to wiggle free, but he held her firm. The water slowly sloshed against the dock, the sun waning in the sky, dipping behind the wall of forest separating the lake from the rest of the world. His mind whirled with a kaleidoscope of lust, doubt, and absolute confidence.

He could make this deal happen. He’d pushed too hard before, assumed too much. Heather wanted more than a contractual obligation from him. He liked her, liked her more than any other person he knew. If she needed more, needed to make the arrangement more than business, he could accommodate her. Hell, there were elements to having a relationship with her he’d thoroughly enjoy.

She stiffened in his grasp, eyeing him warily. Was that why she ran? Did she think he’d expect more than what was on paper from their arrangement? Or was she more afraid that he wouldn’t?

He couldn’t put his finger on what told him it was the latter, but he’d have bet his life savings on it. Maybe Kendra and Mrs. Rutledge were onto something. Maybe all of this happened not because someone had gotten to her, but because her fears had.

“Shouldn’t we go into the house?” she whispered, pulling her bottom lip between her teeth.

“You look amazing today. I didn’t have a chance to tell you before now.” He dropped his hands from her waist, catching her hands in his. Her chest rose as she gasped for breath. He bent his head and grazed her surprised mouth with the kiss he'd wanted to continue earlier.

Damn, but she could kiss. She did everything well, so he didn't know why he was surprised, but she had such an innocent air about her he knew it was a natural talent not a learned skill.

When he kissed her, no matter that she hadn't expected it either time, she completely relaxed. The soft, responsive flesh of her lips convinced him the most important conversation they'd ever have wouldn't contain a single word.

This time alone together would be the perfect opportunity to show her another perk to being the woman on his arm, the side of him that thoroughly enjoyed learning a woman, finding what made her gasp and cry out, moan and purr.

He might not be the Prince Charming of her romantic fantasies, but he wasn't the villain either. He could promise her honesty, fidelity, security, and pleasure.

He pulled back from the kiss, holding her hands until she opened her eyes and took a deep breath. When he released her, she rubbed her fingertips absently against her lips.

Oh, yes, Curtis thought as he picked up the suitcases and started up the path for the house, if that kiss were any indication, everything would work out. Who says you can't mix business with pleasure?

Chapter Six

The cobblestone path leading from the boat dock to the mansion hurt her feet. Curtis trudged ahead, without so much as a backwards glance.

This is what she hated about him, his ability to run ice cold or boiling hot, while she only fluctuated from tepid to simmer. Even the panoramic sweeps of lush forest, smooth lake, and clear sky couldn't turn off her permanent preoccupation with all things Curtis.

Walking behind him, the heavy beaded skirts of her dress in her hands, Heather tried to distract herself with recollections of everything she'd been told about Sapphire Isle and its estate. Her parents had been trying to sell the private island on Lake Shastina for years, but few had the kind of cash to purchase such a sprawling estate, and those who did didn't care to live at the base of Mt. Shasta.

But no one would live here now. They would run the estate as an ultra private resort. The groundskeeper maintained the land, the security team Curtis hired kept an eye on the water, and air flight was restricted in this part of the National Forest. Really, the only way to get here would be to swim.

Once they made it to the foot of the stairs in front of the house, Curtis turned around.

"Golf carts?"

Heather blinked. “Excuse me?”

A smile played on his lips. “I didn’t realize the walk from the dock to the house was this long. The guests aren’t going to want to walk this far.”

“I think it depends on what theme you choose for the resort. Bed-and-breakfast style, they can walk; posh, we’ll find souped-up golf carts; romantic, maybe we’ll have carriages. I have some other ideas too. There is a copy of my report inside the house.”

Tilting his head, he peered down at her. “I thought we were working on this together? You already have it planned out, don’t you?”

She shrugged. “Only the basics. My parents have had the listing on this place for a long time. That’s lots of daydreaming I finally found a use for.”

He smiled, that bone-melting grin, then turned and took the stairs two at a time. With a frustrated huff, Heather looked down at her dress. The hems of the skirts were tinged with dust, but for the most part it held up well. If only she were doing such a good job holding up. The beads were heavy, the skirt cumbersome, the strapless bodice constricting her to perfect posture, and her mental state had deteriorated to a pity party.

“Did I tell you what I think of that dress?” Sarcasm laced his jaded voice. Curtis stood a few steps higher than her, the front door open at the top of the stairs and the suitcases in the foyer. He stared at her, his bright eyes half shuttered, his words shadowed with meaning.

“I said I was sorry.” Her chin trembled under the weight of her emotions. She’d seen her life become perfect, then ruined with one swift turn.

He reached out a hand, but quickly stuffed it in his pocket

and rocked back on his heels. "Heather, I don't want to be walking on eggshells. I don't want everything I say to make you cry. I can't handle tears."

As if she wanted to be an emotional wreck. What she wanted to do right now was hide in one of the nine bedrooms. The house was so big it would take him an hour to find her and she'd have her composure back. She hitched her skirts in her hands and lifted her foot to the first riser.

Muscled arms enveloped her, lifting her off her feet and against Curtis's broad chest. On instinct she clung to his neck, afraid of them both toppling down the stairs as he started up. "What are you doing?"

"Carrying the bride over the threshold. I'm a full-service groom." Once inside, he kicked the door shut and set her gently on her feet. "Now to get you out of that dress."

The dress was gorgeous, no doubt about that. He hadn't given much thought to having a wedding, to how Heather might look. He'd been pleased, proud for those fleeting moments before she turned tail and ran.

He hadn't expected her to transform so completely from secretary to bride. He blinked at the mental hitch. Heather hated to be called his secretary. Executive assistant. Still, she'd always been conservative and wrapped up, hidden behind her glasses and suits. He'd never imagined how sexy her shoulders looked bare, how green her eyes shone, how the curve of a woman's neck could be so impossibly alluring.

The strapless bodice pressed against her breasts, the silk material gathering at her hip then flaring into a full skirt that rioted with sparkling beads. Fantastic, and yet all he wanted to do was get her out of it. He stepped closer, and she backed up all the way to the panel doors closing off one of the living areas.

"I'll do it myself." Her voice went up an octave.

"Are you sure you don't want help?"

She cleared her throat, barely hiding her shudder.

"Heather, I'm not going to do anything you don't want me to."

"I know." The whisper was barely audible, her gaze dropping to the floor.

It took everything in him not to pursue her now. But he'd pushed too fast before, and he didn't want to make the same mistake with her again.

He stepped away, lifting their suitcases. "Are any of the bedrooms made up?"

"The whole house is ready. I wanted you to see how each room was decorated originally."

"Well, which would you like to stay in?"

"I re-did the French room. Second floor, left at the landing."

She started towards the wide mahogany staircase to the left of the foyer. The house was built in the early seventies and decorated with dark woods popular in that time, but flooded with natural light. Desperately in need of redecorating, but they'd agreed to hire someone after they decided on a theme and budget.

"I thought you wanted me to see the rooms as they were?" He fell into step behind her, trying to ignore the swell of her hips as they swung up each riser.

"It was truly horrid. Really, awful."

"But we were planning on having a theme for the resort. Why redecorate one room?" It didn't make sense, and then it did. Maybe she'd planned on sharing the room with him, seducing him while they worked here together, and wanted something nice, not outdated.

"It's just one room. It didn't cost much, really." Heather pushed open the door and stepped inside. Curtis followed, setting the cases inside the door and taking in the room.

From the crystal chandeliers over the bed and sitting area, to the peach walls with cream panels, to the pale blue bedding with ivory fringe on the pillows and bed crown covered in the same material, and beige draperies hugging the bronze bed, it was perfectly put together. Elegant, and yet not so feminine to be off-putting. Exactly what he wished for at home.

"French provincial it is. You sold me."

"I didn't mean it as a sell. I only wanted the room to look nice." Heather turned, holding her hands in front of her. The demure look clenched his gut. She'd wanted this to be her happy ending. He didn't have the heart to tell her they only existed in fairy tales. Especially now, when she looked as if she'd stepped out of the pages of one.

"It's gorgeous. And so are you."

Her cheeks flushed a charming shade of pink. "I don't know what to say."

"Thank you. When someone gives you a compliment, you say thank you."

Heather nodded, wringing her hands.

Comforting her with kisses seemed to be the right thing to do, but he still wasn't sure if it was pushing. Damn. He was used to women with stop and go signals. Heather was all caution and yield.

"It's still early, we should rustle up some dinner and do a tour of the house."

Heather nodded, then started towards the door. He caught her arm. "You need to change. I love the dress, but wearing it all the time is a little too Miss Haversham for me."

One brow arched and she smiled for the first time all day. "*Great Expectations*? I love that book."

So did he. It felt almost like the story of his life. The hidden past, not being who everyone thought you were, pining for perfection. Thankfully he wasn't the idealist Pip was. Reality meant making your own future, not waiting around for someone to dictate it to you.

Except Heather. She'd torn a page out of the book of his life, but it was still up to him to rewrite it. Without letting her down this time.

The bare skin on her arm was warm beneath his touch, the scent of the spiced perfume she wore lilting in the air over the smell of the clean linens. In frustration he dropped his hand. Why was he always trying to push her, rush her?

He shook his head as if to clear it, then walked to her suitcase, lifting it to the mirrored vanity and popping the locks.

"I still think this can work, Heather." He watched her wide-eyed response behind him in the mirrors as he opened the case.

"Even though—"

Her mouth stayed open, but no words emerged as he lifted a pale pink negligee from the case by its ribbon straps. She'd packed lingerie in every color and texture: peach silk, creamy satin, green lace and sheer lilac. A doorknob sign stating *Honeymoon in Progress. Do Not Disturb!* made him wince. Lotions, lubricants and condoms spilled out of a bright pink bag.

Okay, so she hadn't run because she was afraid of his expectations. Hers were much higher. Which could be a very bad thing. If they slept together she might read more into it. He didn't want her to think he loved her when he didn't, just to realize she could have a full and happy life without crashing and burning on the wings of an uncontrollable emotion. Losing his mother had destroyed his father completely, and he'd never cared to open himself up to that prospect.

He met her gaze in the mirror, not the least bit surprised by the crimson blush covering her from the roots of her hair to the bodice of her dress.

"Those aren't mine."

"They should be." In the mirror, his eyes held an ironic gleam.

"No, I mean I didn't buy any of it."

"Too bad. Looks like fun to shop for." He set the lingerie back in the bag and turned to face her.

"But I don't shop for things like that."

"You should." He bit the inside of his cheek to keep from laughing.

Heather pursed her lips together. "I'm not explaining the suitcase very well."

"No, but I am enjoying watching you try."

Heather slapped her hands against the skirt of her dress. "This is an impossible situation. I don't know what it is you want from me, why you're being nice about today, why we're alone together now, why—"

A step forward and a finger on her lips was all it took to silence her. He'd already told her all she wanted to know—he still wanted her, for all the reasons he had before. Nothing had changed, much. His pride stung, but he knew the media well enough to try and salvage the situation in the best way possible.

The fire in her green eyes sparked his curiosity. What would she do if he gave in to the feverish reaction swirling within him? He couldn't risk it, because more than likely the twinkle in her eyes was not a sinful invitation, but the glisten of idealism.

"Let's get you out of your bridal regalia, then we'll talk about it."

"But I don't have anything else to wear, and there isn't much under this." Her lips pulled tight before she erupted into laughter. "I can't believe I'm trapped in a dress."

"We'll get you free in no time." With a hand on her bare shoulder, he moved her in front of him, facing the mirror. "How do I get this out of your hair?" He stared down at the artfully constructed riot of curls with the veil seeming to float out of nothing."

"I couldn't figure that out either."

"Weren't you watching when they did your hair?"

She sighed, her shoulders rising and falling. "No, there was someone putting my face on."

"So you didn't plan on running out."

She pursed her lips together, her glare reflected in the mirror.

"I'm just curious." He found a hairpin and tugged it out.

Heather winced in the mirror. "Or spiteful."

"Spiteful would have been leaving you to the vultures at the marina." Two more hairpins, and her hair still didn't budge. "Here, we can work out what is wrong and be yesterday's news before the month is out."

"Curtis, I can't do it anymore." She wrung her hands, speaking to the floor.

"But you still want to." A few more pins and her hair loosened enough for him to see where the veil erupted from the curls.

"What I want never mattered to you." Anger tightened her features. He jerked the veil out harder than he needed to and set it on the vanity. She'd embarrassed *him*, damn it.

"I provided everything you could ever want, Heather." He'd plucked out all the pins he could find, yet her hair still stayed piled on her head. He shrugged. "At least I got the veil out."

She reached up and tugged her fingers through her hair, the curls falling down around her bare shoulders. "They used a lot of hair products. I think the curls will stay until I wash them out."

"I like it better down." He brushed the locks in front of her shoulder and examined the back of the dress. It looked easier than he expected. It laced up the back, if he could just find where they'd tied the ribbons.

"Wait!" Heather crossed her arms over the bodice of the dress. "What am I going to wear?"

"You have a suitcase full of options I'd love for you to try."

"Be serious."

He met her gaze in the mirror. "I am."

"That would cloud the issue."

"Or clear it up completely."

She rolled her eyes. "You aren't going to seduce me with arguments like that."

"So you can be seduced." He slid his hand beneath her arms, circling her waist and pulling her back against him.

"That might work with the women you usually date, but not with me. I don't know how to play the kind of games you do."

He eased his grip, but didn't let go. "And what kind of games are those?"

"I've read the articles. Seen the pictures."

"I haven't. Enlighten me."

"I know how quickly you tire of the women you sleep with.

And I don't look like they look. Especially with my clothes off."

He chuckled, wrapping both arms around her waist and resting his chin on her shoulder. He met her gaze in the mirror. "I haven't seen as many women naked as you think. And I haven't dated anyone since before you started working for me."

She tried to wriggle away. "What about Christina?"

"The singer? She had an album coming out and an ex-husband in a very public romance with her rival."

"And Patrice? Carmen?"

"Heather. You know Kendra arranged those events with you so they'd fit in my schedule. Do you think I'd let you do that for someone I was interested in?"

"I don't know."

"You didn't arrange dinner when I proposed our arrangement, or when you met my family. And for the record, I'm dying to find out what you look like up close, without the dress."

"I'm not ready for that." Heather raised her gaze to his in the mirror. wishing his sigh didn't sound so much like a groan of frustration.

"I understand." His blue eyes practically glowed.

"No, you don't." She couldn't help but smile. He had a knack for saying the right thing, and not meaning it at all.

"You're right. I don't understand."

"Thank you. Honesty is always appreciated." She huffed a quick breath and looked about the room in the mirror's reflection. "Maybe I could make a toga out of a sheet, or use the curtains."

"Okay, Scarlet." He released her and stepped back, giving her room to breathe—well, breathe as deeply as she could while being tied up in the dress.

She closed her eyes and tried to think of something other than the warm and willing man in the room with her, whose scent filled the air with innuendo. What would it hurt to have a few rounds of hot-and-sweaty, tangled-sheets, down-and-dirty sex with him? Goodness knows they'd both sleep better tonight.

But true to the old adage, she'd hate herself in the morning. She was in love with him, so it would mean something to her. He was negotiating a business deal. His attentions would only last until he got what he wanted, and it wasn't sex.

Telling him what she really wanted from him was akin to emotional suicide. There was nothing she could do except wait out the media frenzy and plan the rest of her life. Once they returned to the real world, Curtis would have nothing to do with her and she'd need all of the pre-planning she could manage to pull free of his sexual energy.

Curtis's fingers against her bare skin opened her eyes. In the mirror his gaze met hers, and he grinned. She swallowed hard at his shirtless reflection. The broad chest, bunching muscles of his shoulders and hard slab of his belly made her want to turn around and examine what was hidden behind her.

She gripped the vanity for support and swallowed again. "What are you doing?"

"I'm taking off your dress, and I'm not looking at you in sheets or drapes. If you don't want to wear what you brought, then you can wear my shirt."

An amorous rush of possibility ignited her imagination. The part of her not intoxicated by his pheromones and lusting after his half-naked body tried to remain in control. She could not sleep with him. Could not.

In the mirror she watched the mischievous gleam in his eye as his hands trailed down the bodice of the dress, then his gaze dropped to his task. The corners of his mouth twitched in a smile he was trying to hide.

Her skin heated, prickling in a blush. She looked at her hands on the top of the vanity to keep from facing the truth. She wanted his hands on her, undressing her, taking whatever he wanted. Her mind's eye showed her his hands as they untied her binds, loosening the laces so she could breathe, but the air was filled with the scent of her longing and his desire.

His hands on her were all she could think of. Until today they'd never been so intimate. It was like something out of a storybook, where all physicality was saved for after the marriage. Except she hadn't married him. She hadn't saved herself for marriage either.

"Curtis—"

"Do I pull it over your head, or do you step out of it?"

"Over my head." If that wasn't the truth.

"Hands up, then."

She raised her hands above her head, the bodice lifting up and over, followed by the billowing skirts. She heard the gown rustle as he tossed it on the chaise behind them. Quickly, she wrapped one arm across her bare breasts and reached for his shirt. The soft cotton slipped in her fingers.

"Can you wait?" The words were barely a whisper.

Heather caught a glimpse of his face in the mirror and her stomach flipped at his reaction. He stared at her nearly nude body, one knuckle pressed between his teeth. Power flooded her. She'd done that to him, made him want to stare. He was looking at her, seeing her as something other than employee, and he liked what he saw. Well, he liked the bridal thong she wore, with a veil covering her bottom. She grinned at her newfound ability. In the mirror, his eyes met hers.

She shook her head slightly, to let him know she hadn't

changed her mind. He nodded and stepped closer, delicious longing bolting through her body like lightning.

Her imagination ran like a cheetah, wild and free. He was hers for the taking, hers to have and hold, even if it was only while they were here, waiting out the bloodhounds. If loving him was going to be her one great regret, she really ought to have something to lament.

Curtis leaned closer, his mouth grazing her earlobe, his hand firm on the soft flesh of her hip. “You are so beautiful.” His voice, rich and resonant, made her quiver.

His muscled arm snaked around her middle, pulling her flush against him. He nipped at her ear, pulling her lobe between his teeth, his hot breath sending prickles down her arm, which shifted involuntarily, baring her breasts to the mirror.

His pupils widened, darkening his eyes as he eyed her beaded nipples. She stole a glance at him beneath her eyelashes, unsure what she was supposed to do. Sex to her had always been in a bed, in the dark. This openness was completely new, and more than a little thrilling.

The urge to protect her heart and run battled with the anticipation of staying. Her skin thrummed at the possibility. His hand dipped from her hip, firm against the pliant flesh of her belly. As his hand trailed lower, her gaze came back into focus and she saw herself in the mirror. Hippy, chubby Heather, nearly naked in the mirror, standing in front of one of the most perfect male specimens ever created. She stiffened, reaching for the shirt.

“Don’t.” The gravel in his voice made her want to obey.

“I have to.” She wriggled free, wrapping the deep blue shirt around her body and fastening the buttons with trembling hands.

"You don't *have* to."

"This isn't a game for me, Curtis. I don't want you to manipulate me or pity me."

"Pity you?"

"I know I don't look like the women you're usually with. The models and singers and—"

He spun her around, knocking her off balance as he pulled her face to face with him by her shoulders. "I don't want them."

She found her feet, trying to break free of him, but he pinned her with his gaze. "Find someone else to play the fiancée. Someone who is a better actress."

"I want out of that world, Heather. I want people to see me for what I do, not for who I date or where I go on vacation. I want out. I want a normal life."

She almost felt sorry for him, pretty little rich boy terrorized by the media. Except, she realized why he chose her. Not because he trusted her like she thought, but because she wasn't picture perfect, she wasn't interesting to the tabloids, she wasn't anything to him but a ticket out of the spotlight and straight to the land of dull and boring. How insulting.

"You deserve more." *I deserve more.*

"I have more than enough."

"You don't have love." Liar. Her conscience flared like a viper about to strike. She loved him, madly, deeply. If she stayed with him he would have that for the rest of her life.

"There are lots of different kinds of love."

"Do you love me?" She clenched her jaw to keep her chin from trembling.

He held her gaze. "No."

"Then why me? Why not one of the other women in your life?"

"There aren't people in my life, Heather."

"What about Kendra? She knows the game."

"She ought to, she wrote the rules." He had the nerve to smile. "There is no one who knows me better than you do. This is a great move for you. You won't have to worry about money ever again. You understand about my work, you realize how important it is that I be seen as more than a playboy, be taken seriously."

She nodded. She realized a lot. He'd chosen her because he thought she should be grateful, should think a guaranteed income was a good trade for her time spent smiling on the arm of a man who had upgraded her from assistant in name only. In his reality, she'd be a secretary with special benefits.

Her skin chilled at the thought. She'd almost slept with him tonight, almost handed what was left of her dignity to a man who calculated her worth in dollars and cents. She'd been right to run.

All her life she'd been looking for her prince to come and save her from the world of mediocrity. But Curtis Frye wasn't a prince, wasn't looking for someone to love him as deeply as he loved. He might be able to set her soul on fire, but his heart was stuck on freeze.

"You know why I ran, Curtis?"

He shook his head.

"I was standing in the middle of my dream, with the man I love." She reached up and brushed away a tear with her finger. "But you feel nothing for me. Until that moment I thought I could make it happen. I thought if we were together you'd come around. But I saw you in that church, getting everything you wanted, and realized I was getting nothing in return."

"Heather, you agreed to the terms-"

She held up her hand, tired of the pretense. “I won’t be with a man who doesn’t love me, no matter what it costs.”

Chapter Seven

Curtis tried not to laugh, but she was being ridiculously naïve. “You didn’t agree to our arrangement because you were in love.”

“Yes, I did.” Her eyes glistened like jade, murky and deep.

“You’re kidding yourself. It wasn’t me you agreed to, it was the money, the glamour, the lifestyle.”

“You can stuff your lifestyle, Curtis. Even you don’t like it.” She stiffened, her face rushing bright red. “I am not a gold digger.”

“Sure you are. It’s fine, everybody is.”

“Not me!”

He rolled his eyes. She was in complete denial. “Just look at the planning you were doing for a non-existent wedding.”

She pointed a finger at him. “That was your mother, not me. That had nothing to do with why I agreed.”

He stepped towards her, reaching for her hands, but she wrapped her arms across her body. “Don’t get defensive. I wanted you to feel like Cinderella. But you do know fairy tales aren’t reality. Just like those articles about me, they’re all fabrications.”

“I know that.” She spat the words at him, her green eyes narrowing. She brushed the vine-like tendrils of her hair over her shoulder.

"Then why are you so angry?"

"Because you think you know me. You assume you know what I am thinking. And if you believe I did this for the money, then you don't know the first thing about me."

"I'm a quick study. You imagine for a relationship to work, you have to have some magical connection, that love is the answer for all your problems. Even in the best relationships, love is secondary at best. Compatibility, shared goals, respect and attraction are all more important. We have that."

He lifted a hand to her hair, pulling a tendril back in front of her shoulder. Standing so close to her, he couldn't help but remember what it was like to hold her in his arms, have her full lips against his, her lush curves pressed against him. He bent his head, barely grazing her surprised mouth with a kiss.

"We need each other, Heather. And love has nothing to do with it."

"I don't need you. *You* need *me.*" She tilted her chin up, staring him in the eye. The lusty, full-bodied tone of her voice nearly paralyzed his logic. "I can walk away from this and start over. You'll have to find someone willing to settle for a life without love and romance."

Her tongue darted out, wetting her lips. Curtis bit back the need to kiss her again. He could tell she felt the same attraction he did, and with the slightest push they'd both tumble into bed, hopefully staying there for a few days until this lust-induced fog cleared.

"I never said we wouldn't have romance. Passion, adventure, mind-blowing sex." He reached for her face, his fingers against her cheek, the pad of his thumb brushing across her ripe lips.

"I can't separate it the way you can."

"You want me, Heather. Don't start lying to me now."

"I'm not saying you don't turn me on. I'm saying that it's not because of how we are together physically. I love you, and that is what makes me want to be with you, to have more of you."

"You can have as much of me as you can take." His hand drifted from her face, to her earlobe, then down her neck to the second-from-the-top button of his shirt. He was tired of his shirt getting to feel more of her than he had, and flicked the button open with one hand.

Her hand closed over his. "I don't want you if I can't have it all. I won't settle for sex when I can have lovemaking, accept friendship when I can have passion. We both deserve more than a business arrangement."

Lying to her, saying he would love her, was so tempting. His cock twitched at the thought of calling her bluff, taking her to the bed and working everything out without words. But he'd long ago realized love was too powerful an emotion to allow into his heart. He couldn't bring himself to break his own rules to bend her will.

He saw it clearly from her side, the world of happily ever after and promises to keep. But he'd lived a different life, knew there was a dark side to love that could drive a man to lose himself, knew he could never give himself completely to another person. Not even someone he trusted as much as Heather.

Two strong-willed people with two equally correct views of reality might never see eye to eye. And yet he wasn't ready to give in. They were here, alone. That gave them the chance to find some middle ground, or enjoy themselves trying.

"I want you to have all you deserve, Heather." He framed her face in his hands, and reveled from the beauty that glowed from the inside. The kind that would never fade. "Let me show you I'm the man to give it to you."

She squeezed her eyes shut, shrinking from him. "I don't want you to keep kissing me."

"Yes you do." He stepped closer, sweeping her hair over her shoulder and bending to nuzzle her neck. The apples-and-cinnamon scent she wore warmed his lungs.

"It gives you the wrong idea about what I want." Despite her protests, she tilted her head, giving him better access. "That's why I didn't want to put on any of the lingerie."

His lips pulled at her earlobe, his hands drifting down her body to her full bottom and squeezing until she shivered. He blew a hot breath against her ear, then whispered, "The sexiest thing you'll ever wear, is me. And the next best thing, is my shirt."

He released her, stepping towards the door. He turned back, taking in the shocked look in her eyes, the uncontrolled curls in her hair, his shirt unbuttoned to the middle of her chest, her legs long and shapely beneath the hem.

He sucked in a sharp breath, his erection growing painful. "You might as well lose the panties now, Heather. We're inevitable."

The arrogance of the man shouldn't be attractive. Heather pawed through the suitcase, looking for anything useful. She'd switched from the ridiculous bridal thong her sister insisted on. When she'd opened the gift, they'd all laughed until tears came from their eyes, and of course dared her to wear it today. Now she was stuck with a butt veil, and *bride* embroidered in baby blue on the front of her sheer white panties.

The ruffled pair of boy shorts was the best she could manage. At least her toiletry bag was in the case, along with the longest roll of condoms known to man. Really, those women needed a hobby.

Buttoning up Curtis's shirt, she made her way downstairs to a kitchen the size of her entire apartment. She'd had her roommates create a dozen meals for them in case Curtis got as in the zone about the estate as he did the rest of his projects. She'd thought they might end up staying a few days, and wanted to be prepared. Tugging open the enormous fridge, she pulled out one of the containers, and poured the contents into a pot according to the directions on the top. The crab and sweet corn chowder only needed to be heated through, then poured into the bread bowls also in the fridge. She set the bread in the oven to warm and rifled through the cupboard she'd stocked with plates, utensils, glasses and of course wine.

Except she'd forgotten to pack a wine opener. With a frustrated huff, she shrank back against the counter. She really needed a drink. She'd run out on her own bridal photo shoot, was being pursued by the paparazzi, and was hiding out on a private island with the man of her dreams.

The smile tightened her cheeks. Curtis Frye was alone in a house with her, and he'd made it clear he'd do anything she liked between the sheets. She was a glass-is-half-full kind of girl, but if she wasn't careful she'd romanticize everything again and be in over her head. She really needed to look at this situation from the other side.

Curtis wasn't going to be her future. She wasn't willing to sign away her soul for a marriage, even if it was to the man she loved. He didn't love her, but he was attracted to her. The story of her life.

She'd always tried to make relationships work,

compromising parts of herself for a future with men who didn't think further than next month. That was one of the things that attracted her to Curtis. The man had a five-year plan written in stone. Well, he did until she chiseled out her name.

She'd been guilty of exactly what he was doing—making the most out of an almost-perfect situation. Her college boyfriend had been persuaded into a trip to Mexico to give him the perfect location to propose, until he didn't. She always had a hard time knowing when to let go. She'd learned the hard way there was no point trying to jumpstart a relationship once the battery had gone dead.

Except this didn't feel dead. They'd barely turned the key. But she didn't know how she could be with him knowing they could never be together. Though she knew it would be a huge regret if she never made him hers, if only for a few days.

"You wrote the entire business plan." Curtis appeared out of nowhere, slamming a red folder on the granite countertop. "It's complete. Better than the last few plans I received from project managers. Why didn't you tell me you knew how to do this?"

He grabbed the bottle from her hands, marching out of the kitchen before she could respond. She'd done her best on the plan to transform the estate into a resort, wanting to make sure they had ample time for other things, more sensual things, but she'd never thought it would be good enough on its own.

Before she could get her wits about her, he was back, handing her the uncorked bottle of Pinot Grigio.

"How did you do that?"

"There's a bottle opener mounted to the bar in the living room. I've been showing myself around. That's how I found your plan."

Instead of answering, she poured the wine into the glasses

she'd found and took a healthy gulp.

"When did you have time to research a plan like that?"

"I told you that I've been thinking about this place since my parents listed it." The wine was cool and mellow, perfect for soothing her nerves.

"The designer-themed rooms are a great idea, and a good way to keep costs down. Designers are doing collections for stores all over the place. It will be easy to order the items and set the rooms up quickly."

Easy for him, since she'd been the one scouting the collections at different department stores, finding which ones worked. Arranging setup and delivery on an island that only offered boat access was another story entirely. Setting up the bedroom had been a logistics tangle.

"Do you really think this place could be operational in three months?"

"It would take some doing, but yes." She finished her glass of wine and poured a second. She hadn't eaten anything all day. Her stomach and nerves demanded nothing take precedence over dinner.

"I'd like for you to manage the project, devote yourself to this venture. We'll present it to the hospitality group. They can begin recruiting for the staff and start marketing it." Curtis merely swirled his wine in the glass, staring off into space.

She set her glass down, removed the bread bowls from the oven and set them on plates. She needed food and he needed a hefty dose of reality.

"I doubt I'll be working for you next week."

"Why not?" He slammed the wineglass against the counter so hard she feared the stem might break.

"Shall I rewind the events of the day for you? We were

standing at the altar of a church, and I turned around and ran."

"Leaving your shoes behind." He stalked closer to her, the look in his eye fierce and predatory. She busied herself with the now-steaming soup, pouring it into the bread bowls, ignoring his closeness.

"You try running in them."

"Not my thing, though you in the heels and nothing else would earn my forgiveness."

"I'm not interested." She slid a spoon onto the plate, then balanced it in one hand and took her wine in another, making her way outside to the veranda. Once outside, she let the sweeping expanse of sky, mountain and water calm her.

With the sun growing tired, the lake darkened to a deep sapphire, the shoreline reddening as an echo to the pink tingeing the sky. Solitude rang out from the rise of Mount Shasta, the mountain ascending so high it was still streaked with snow, even this late in the summer. Fluttering with birds of every type and stands of cedar, sequoia and pine, the mountain was as beautiful as the air was crisp and clean.

The world around the island was so pure, she wondered if transforming the estate into a resort would taint it. She filled her lungs with a soothing breath of fresh air, loving the scent of it. If she remained in charge of the project, she could ensure the quiet and innocence of the land were what they prided themselves on. It was what high-end clientele lacked most. If they wanted to party, let them go to places that did that better than she could ever envision. This would be a place of relaxation and rejuvenation. Healing for the weariest souls.

The sweet creaminess of the soup warmed her mouth as her body chilled. She couldn't protect the project if she didn't give in and stay with Curtis. She'd not only be fired, but likely blackballed from the entire community. Maybe she ought to skip dinner and go straight for the ice cream she'd stocked for dessert and other emergencies. She needed an IV of chocolate to numb her from the realization that in choosing herself, she'd abandoned everything else.

Especially Curtis. There was no telling who he would elect to be his next fiancée, what they would want from him in return.

"This is romantic." Curtis drifted onto the veranda, his plate in one hand, wineglass in the other. A corked bottle of wine rested in the crook of his elbow.

She looked around, smiling at the implication. "Romance is inherent in the location. Really, the less you do to the house the better it will be."

"I was talking about you, making dinner to eat while we watch the sun set on the water. It's very romantic." He slid into the chair opposite her at the table, setting the wine between them and pulling out the cork. "It took me a bit to find where you're keeping the wine, though."

He refilled her glass and she lifted it, staring at the pale gold liquid that had finally begun to take the edge off her nerves. His bare foot slid against hers beneath the table, and she didn't move away. She couldn't help but wonder if she shouldn't at least taste what it was she was giving up, before her conscience required her to return everything in the name of her stupid pride.

"You have a beautiful smile. I've always thought your face wasn't made to frown."

Her smile widened. "What does that mean?"

"When you smile, you are breathtaking. When you cry—"

"I know. It's ugly."

"That's the wrong word. It is just so sad to go from perfect to destroyed."

"I destroy my face when I cry?" She giggled, glad for the release.

"I'm not good with words."

"You were pretty spectacular with them earlier." She rubbed her foot against his and sipped her wine.

"And still you denied me. You have a will of iron, Heather Tindall."

If only. Right now she didn't know if it was the wine, the sky painted in pinks and oranges, or the fresh air that made her want to take him up on every naughty offer he'd made earlier. If she was going to give him up, she should have something to remember him by. Something like days of making love to him until he couldn't see straight.

"Now *that* is a smile." The waning light reflected off his dark hair, coating everything in a warm pink haze.

"Just daydreaming." She set her empty wineglass down, twirling a curl around her finger. Whether she was drunk on the sunset, his pheromones or the wine, she didn't know. But the anxious side of her decided to turn in for the night, leaving her completely relaxed and peaceful for the first time in months.

"About?"

She stretched in her seat, looking out past the deck to the pool below. The cool water against her skin would feel decadent right now. She looked at Curtis as she rose from her chair, stretching again.

"Sex." The husky voice didn't surprise her. She didn't feel much like herself anyway. Fragments of thought flitted through her head, visions of dreams, but nothing solidified. Nothing compared to reality.

Her desire for him was so powerful it was tangible, like a

cord tethering them together. Never had she been overwhelmed with desire to the point of recklessness, but with her body a snarl of excited nerves she didn't see any way to soothe them but to give in to the pleasure promised in his leering gaze.

"Why waste time dreaming when you can make it happen?" His low voice vibrated across her skin.

"Because I'm not going to agree to our arrangement, and you think sex will make me want to." She stepped to the railing of the deck, looking out at the sun, flaming red as it dipped low, as if Lake Shastina were swallowing it up.

She was so tired of fighting with him, of them each thinking making love might change things. As if good sex could make him fall in love with her when he never intended to, or make her sell her soul for flashy vacations and expensive dinners. Really, the only way to put this whole sordid chapter of their lives behind them would be to remove the bargaining chip.

For so long she'd struggled with her feelings, riding the roller coaster of hope until she opted off the ride this morning. She'd fought to wipe out the want, negate the need, demolish the desire—to no avail. Even after all that had happened, she still craved his touch, yearned to know him in the most primal way.

She wrapped her fingers around the railing, wondering if it could possibly be any harder to let him go once they'd made love. Wouldn't it be better to love him fully, completely, if only for a moment?

Curtis cleared his throat, but when he spoke it still sounded gravelly. "We don't have to do anything you don't want to do. But it is probably the only way either of us will get any sleep tonight."

She turned her head, noticing the smile that didn't quite make it to his eyes. In the last year she'd spent studying him, she'd never seen him look so on the brink of losing control. He was always in control, always knew the answer before he asked the question. But today she'd pulled the rug clean out from under him. Good. It was only fair after the off-kilter way she felt around him every day.

"There are other ways to burn off your frustrations." She released the railing and what was left of her moral high ground. She knew what she wanted to do, and by the hungry look in his eye, seducing him would be a breeze.

The stairs down to the pool weren't steep, yet she held the handrail for balance as her mind whirled with all the things she'd forgotten. A swimsuit, towel, protection. Part of their contract had involved a complete physical, and came with a birth-control shot—so she could relax on one of the three. She'd thought the birth control a bit much at the time, but when he explained he couldn't have her getting pregnant by someone else when she was supposed to be engaged to him, it became comical. As if she'd be doing this if she could imagine herself with anyone but Curtis.

As she reached the pool, the lights of the house came on behind her, brightening the area. She hadn't even thought about that, how she would manage to find the stairs again in the dark. Well, if she wasn't thinking straight, best to go all out.

She turned back towards the deck, but saw no one there. She plucked at the buttons of Curtis's shirt, searching for his silhouette in the windows. "Aren't you going to come with me?"

"Ladies first."

Chapter Eight

The house cloaked him in shadow beside the stairs, allowing him to watch Heather search for him as she unbuttoned her shirt. His shirt. His erection strained against his jeans, reminding him he wouldn't be able to hide much longer. His desire for her burned like a hunger, calling for him to sate his need.

Never had a woman been this potent to him, driven him to this teetering precipice of desire. She'd had him off-kilter since she ran out of the church. If she loved him like she claimed, she wouldn't have run. It wasn't logical.

Neither was the intense attraction that surged when she shrugged off the shirt and laid it on the lounge. The ruffled white panties covering her round bottom made his cock twitch. The water in that pool had better be damned cold, or he'd lose it before he even had the chance to touch her.

She tugged the panties from her hips, bending over to pull them off the rest of the way. Long legs stepped gracefully poolside, the glorious curves of her body flowing from her full hips to her narrower waist. Her dark hair cascaded over her shoulders, hiding her breasts as she turned sideways, surveying the water.

With a gentle arc to her body, she dove into the water and swam the length of the pool beneath the surface. Instead of emerging at the opposite end, she did a half-somersault, then twisted her body, pushing off the wall and propelling herself forward at full speed.

She surfaced in the middle of the pool, water streaming from her hair, highlighting the smooth curves of her face. She dipped her head back, her hair slicking to her scalp.

"You can come in, Curtis." A cheeky smirk played on her pretty lips. She'd known he was watching all along.

She swam around playfully, her moves slow and deliberate, her long legs spreading apart, then coming together so that beneath the distortion of the water he couldn't see as much of her as he needed. Yet he couldn't move, mesmerized by the beauty of her naked body and the darkness gradually enveloping them.

Lying on her back, she floated on the surface, her bareness finally exposed to him, wearing nothing but her tight, pink nipples. Water flowed between her lush breasts, making them islands like the one they were on.

Blood rushed through his veins, his pulse pounding in his ears, chest, groin until he felt overcome by his lust for her. He'd never had his libido overpower his senses in this way, not even as a teenager. Now, all he could see was Heather's body bare for him, feel her kiss from earlier still on his lips, crave the taste of her on his tongue, the feel of her soft skin beneath his hands, and the sound of the water sloshing in the pool, calling him.

The logical part of his mind reminded him this was Heather who sat in his front office every day dressed all in black, who hid behind glasses and drowned her frustrations in blended coffee drinks. He knew her as something other than this wanton goddess, and yet the knowledge couldn't rein in his desire.

He wanted to have her in every way possible. Her ripe breasts beneath his palms, her budded nipple on his tongue, her lush thighs wrapped around his body, giving him complete access to her everywhere.

With all the blood in his body surging south, he had trouble getting his fingers to undo his belt, unfasten his jeans. He leaned on the side of the stairs for support as he stepped out of his pants and carefully pulled off his briefs. His body ached for her so deeply it hurt. How was once going to be enough? It would take more than a night, more than this week to soothe the pain.

Heather had been the perfect choice for a wife because she was the logical option. Trustworthy, dependable, respected. But she was also the only woman who came to mind when he thought of whom he might marry. No one else even entered his brain. As he stepped from the shadows he wondered if this was why. If a part of him knew this sensuous side of her lurked beneath the sass and stability.

He liked this side, but he liked the others too. The way she wouldn't take flak from anyone, even him. The way she committed to a task and saw it through with complete dedication. Until today, he hadn't realized he'd rushed her into a façade of a relationship without ever considering all it could be.

He'd been willing to settle for a business partnership, but now he saw they could be so much more. Friends, lovers, partners. It was more of a risk than he'd bargained for at first, but he cared about Heather, cared enough to meet her half way. He had to keep her. Letting her go wasn't an option.

Stepping to the edge of the pool, he stared down at her, wondering what she thought of as she languidly floated on the surface. Did she ache for him the way he did for her? Laughter bubbled up in his chest. It wasn't possible.

Heather shifted, moving to stand in the water. The

moonlight waxing in the distance made her green eyes glow, droplets of water still on her dark eyelashes. Her lips spread in a grin, growing wicked and hungry as her gaze devoured his body inch by inch.

The water lapped at her body like a hypnotic haze, soothing her desire, drawing out her every sensual reaction. Nearly weightless in the water, she stared up at him, his light eyes shining an intense aquamarine that punctuated the hunger in his gaze. He stood above her, so big, male and mesmerizing that she couldn't take her eyes off him. His defined chest with a fine spray of dark hair trailing over his flat stomach and lower... She dragged her gaze back up his body, meeting his eyes once more. The only thing that would make him look better would to be dripping wet.

She floated back a little to cooler water. The water heated at the sight of him. She was deep under the spell of the sensations of the currents pushing around her, reacting to her every movement, luxuriating in the arousal.

"You should join me."

"I will." He looked at the far end of the pool, then back at her.

"What are you waiting for?"

"I'm trying to think of the best way to get in."

"What is it? Can't you swim?" She splashed at him playfully, slightly worried she might have hit the mark.

"Oh, that's how it is?" He smiled down at her, warm and wicked. He took one step back, then cannonballed into the pool, sending water flying everywhere. Heather ducked down to avoid the spray, but Curtis beat her beneath the surface, his hands on either side of her face as he pulled her to him, their lips meeting in an underwater kiss.

She gave herself over to the exhilaration, parting her lips slightly as he kissed her, their bodies floating together as their lips met without friction. Breaking the lip lock, he released her, leaving her alone to break the surface.

Stunned by the kiss, she treaded to where she could anchor her feet on the pool floor, her head and neck above water. She'd made a silly list of fifty things to do in her life back in college, and kissing underwater was right below skinny-dipping in the moonlight. She hadn't thought of the list in years, until he was kissing her, making her wishes come true. Two for two on the day.

Water slid off her hair, across her face, as she tried to find her bearings. This felt real, yet maybe it was a vivid dream. The items on the list sped through her mind.

Fall madly in love. She was crazy to be in love with him, that's for sure.

Have a fairy tale wedding. Almost got that one too.

Water rippled behind her, warning her before Curtis was there, sliding up her body so close she could feel the heat coming off him without him even touching her. One large hand snaked around her middle, pulling her back against him, so near she felt every muscle of his hard body, including the straining erection at the small of her back.

"I didn't mean to scare you," he whispered against her ear, nuzzling her neck.

"You didn't." Her hand drifted down, against his firm thigh, the sparse hair the only friction between them. "I just remembered something."

"What?" He peppered her neck and shoulder with hot kisses, the warmth moving down her body, anticipation building between her thighs.

"I made a list of things I want to do."

"Am I on it?"

She couldn't help but laugh, looking through the water to watch his hands drift up her body until they palmed her breasts. Having his hands there eased the ache, until he started to caress her and it began to build again.

"Am I the only thing on it?"

"You are so arrogant." His laugh vibrated the water around them, turning her desire up another degree. "I wrote it before we met, in college. I haven't thought of it since."

She couldn't stifle a moan as he expertly caressed her breasts, his fingers attending to her beaded nipples. She rested her head back against his shoulder, letting him support her before she continued.

"Skinny dipping in the moonlight was on the list, but I didn't think of it until you kissed me underwater."

"I didn't think it would take my breath away. We can try it again tomorrow. Right now I am too worked up." He ground his erection against her back in emphasis. One of his hands snaked lower, cupping her mound. "Forget everything. It will be there tomorrow."

He was right. Reality never left, but fantasy was fleeting. "I wanted to kiss in the rain too, and beneath a waterfall."

She turned easily in his embrace, the water making her slippery and slick. Her arms went naturally around his neck, his chest hair teasing her tight nipples as she pressed against him. He took her lips between his, capturing them in a heated, promising kiss. She barely noticed as he lifted her up, her feet drifting as he moved them to the side of the pool, pressing her up against the wall. He pulled his lips away, taking her breasts in his hands.

"I wanted to make love in a pool."

He grinned, wicked and dark, before dipping his head to run his tongue around the hardened bud of her nipple.

"And on the beach."

He flicked his tongue across the peak, his other hand attending to her other breast.

"And in the rain."

Again he rewarded her with more attentions, more pleasure.

"A bed of roses."

She tried desperately to remember the list, to keep the pleasure coming at a steady stream. "On a train. Under the stars." She writhed against his onslaught. "On a yacht. A rooftop. On the grass."

Oh sweet heaven, he switched to the other breast and she was done with that part of her list. She closed her eyes and envisioned all the places she'd ever wanted to knock him to the ground and take him.

"On your desk." The moaning need in her voice must belong to someone else. "In your bed."

"Yours is better." He barely moved, the tension swirling deep in her belly.

"It is?"

"Trust me." He played with her breast with one hand, the other roaming her body, awakening all her sensations. "Is that all?" he asked, barely letting up. "Because we can have that done before the end of the week."

Think. It was nearly impossible when she was about to come undone. "On the kitchen table."

"In every room of that house."

"The house is huge." She undulated against him, fighting the urge to wrap her leg around his back and grind against him to find her release.

"It will barely take the edge off." His hand slithered down her body, cupping her bottom and pressing his erection against her.

He had a point. She had nearly a year of frustration to work out. The house was just the beginning. "On a trampoline."

He released her breast, straightening up. "Where do we get a trampoline?"

She was not thinking logically just now. "I was fantasizing."

He shook his head. "This is a planning session. You want love, Heather, we'll make it."

He caught her mouth, trapping her in a kiss before she could explain that wasn't what she'd meant by love. But she knew it was the best he had to offer, the closest she'd come to having him love her. And while it wasn't nearly enough for a lifetime, it was enough for a night.

With her arms wrapped around his neck, her hardened nipples pressing mercilessly against his chest, her mouth hot and insistent beneath his, he pressed his dick against her warm body. The slide against her supple flesh made him even harder.

She released her grasp on his neck as he pushed her back into the wall, thinking of nothing but finding the release they both needed so desperately. No one held the upper hand here, the desire between them might have ignited into flames if they weren't underwater.

Soft hands slid over his shoulders, down his chest, reaching between them. Her fingers found the little separation, grasping his cock. She stroked him, slow and sure, moaning into his mouth.

The time for waiting was past them, but he knew water was

not a friend to lovemaking. As much as he wanted to take her now, he knew the only way to get them both there was to be slow. Maybe she'd opted for the pool and skinny-dipping just to drive him mad with lust. What a beautiful idea.

Lifting her off her feet, he turned them around so he had his back to the pool wall. He reached one hand down to her sex, finding her lips plump and engorged, ready for him. He teased one finger between, her entry slick and pulsing. She lifted one leg, and he grabbed for the other, crossing them behind his back.

A thrill shot down his spine as she stretched her hands across his chest, her thumbs circling his nipples. With a low groan he gripped her bottom, pressing his hardness against her willing entrance.

He gently lowered her onto his shaft, using every ounce of control he still had. Her hands crept to his shoulders, her mouth working his tense neck, the long vines of her hair wet against his cheek.

She was weightless in the water, allowing him to lift her up and down on his shaft while her hot mouth seared against his skin. With a moan she pulled her lips away, arching her body backward. Her flushed skin told of her arousal, but the flicker in her bright green eyes let him know she had still more in store for him.

His body had awakened to her touch, with just her passion-filled stare the response intensified deep inside him. She arched back until her head lay on the surface of the water, her body floating weightless for his pleasure. She anchored one of her hands on his elbow as she rocked against him.

"More, Curtis." Her throaty demand was all the encouragement he needed.

Her body undulated with each thrust, the water rippling

around them in the most erotic display he'd ever seen. That it was actually happening, to him, to them, nearly had him at the edge. It would have plunged him over if Heather hadn't arched farther, her face disappearing beneath the surface of the water.

Water rushed over her face as she emerged, gasps for breath mixing with the sounds of pleasure. She taunted him this way, dipping back under the water until he was straining against his own release, too driven by his cascading desire to hold back much longer.

With her leaning back, their joining was exposed to him, her clit ripe and full. He circled it, pressing lightly, but it only served to send her arching deeper into the pool. He quickened his pace, both with his hand and his cock, determined not to have her be the first woman to outlast him. Not now, not ever.

She shot up out of the water, gasping and shrieking his name into the still night. Her fingernails dug into his shoulders as her body began to shudder and quake. The tight spasms pulled his orgasm from him, his world narrowing as every nerve in his body exploded like a ball of lightning. The ache in his groin emptied into her, dispelling his frustrations and fears.

She held him close, still quivering with the intensity of their coupling. They'd burned so hot he felt as though they'd melted together, permanently fusing to the other. He felt taut and vibrant, yet as calm as he could ever recall.

He rubbed a hand up her back, the bumps of her spine tickling his palm. "That was—"

"What I was afraid of." She tried to wrench herself from him, but he grabbed her by the shoulders, looking into her tear-filled eyes.

"I hurt you?" He shifted, removing himself from her body, the cool water shocking his system.

She shook her head, worrying her bottom lip between her

teeth. "I knew it would be like this. You and me. I thought if it wasn't then—"

"It's always like that for you?" They'd never get anything done again. Hell, they should move here and lock out the rest of the world forever.

"No. I told you, it's like this because—"

"Heather, it was amazing." He cleared his throat, unwilling to listen to her professions of love while his synapses were still scrambled. "But—"

She covered his mouth with her hand. "Don't say that now. Not right now, okay? Because if you would only let yourself feel something, anything, I think it would be for me."

Chapter Nine

He'd ruined everything. In her experience, men liked to have sex and then shut up about it. Not Curtis, no. He had to go and try to rationalize emotions. *What a crock.*

Back in her room, Heather rifled through her suitcase, looking for anything that resembled clothing. She should have grabbed his shirt off the lounger when she stomped her way back to the house, but she'd only been thinking of the way he dropped his gaze, shutting her out when she challenged him.

There was no breaking down walls that well-built. The best he had to offer was peeks through his armor, and that wasn't a relationship. She fisted the lace of a teddy in anger, slamming it to the floor. *So unfulfilling.* She really ought to throw something that made a sound when it landed.

Finally, she uncovered a silk chemise with a matching robe. Neither covered her thighs, but two layers were better than nudity. She'd thought of trying to find where Curtis had stashed his case and stealing another shirt, but the chances of being caught and having to face him while she was still so raw were too high.

Tightening the sash of the robe, she tiptoed out of her room and down the darkened hallway to the kitchen. There wasn't much clean-up to do, just soaking the pot she'd heated the soup in and collecting their dinner dishes. She stared at the windows facing the pool. The still surface of the water meant he wasn't there, but she didn't know where he'd run off to, or what he was planning. Curtis Frye always had a plan. She usually loved the way nothing ever held him back, but now that his skillfulness might be turned on her, she hated nothing more.

Her body felt torn in two, her head demanding she stand her ground and hold on to her pride, but everything from her heart down told her to take what he offered. No point holding out for something he didn't even have to give.

Heather walked to the windows, pulling her hair over her shoulder and twisting it into a braid as she looked for him in the pool, the hot tub. Nothing. She didn't want to face him, but she didn't like the guilt she felt at having basically told him he was an iceberg. Even if it was true, she knew by the way he wouldn't meet her gaze that she'd hurt him. Somewhere.

Good girls should not try and tempt bad boys. Not ever. They didn't play by the same rules, so someone always ended up hurt. Curtis never accepted defeat as an option, so he'd keep pushing until she relented, and since she'd rather die than live a lie, they'd run the other into the ground until they were two pools of jelly.

Good gravy. *That* would make the tabloids.

Finally finding a smile, Heather pushed open the sliding glass doors and stepped onto the terrace. A slight breeze blew, but not enough to take the heat from the air.

"You want to know what I think?" Curtis's voice rumbled from a blackened section of the deck.

Heather nearly tossed the plate she held, her startled heartbeat galloping away. "You scared me."

"I think you're being naive." His voice continued, though she still couldn't tell from where. "If you polled a hundred women, I think you'd find they'd all envy your position. And I'd bet most women marry with less going for them than we have."

"Stop!" Stacking the plates, Heather turned to the sound of his voice, barely making out the outline of him sitting in a chair, his feet propped on one of the end tables. "You can stop trying to sell me on something, because I am not buying. And for your information, if I surveyed a hundred women, they'd all tell me to hightail it away from you."

She grabbed the dishes and marched back into the kitchen, then set them in the sudsy water already in the sink. Deciding she'd leave them for tomorrow, she pulled open the freezer and grabbed a pint of ice cream. Coffee with swirls of caramel and fudge. Rummaging through a drawer, she found a spoon and pried the lid off the container.

"Why?" Curtis stood silhouetted by the windows, sliding the glass door closed. He'd put his pants back on, and slipped the shirt he'd loaned her earlier around his shoulders, not bothering to button it. "I'm ideal husband material."

"Ha!" Heather pointed her spoon at him. "You have serious commitment issues. You—"

"I'm completely committed to you. Do you want a longer time frame on the agreement? Consider it done."

"I am not negotiating with you." She took a bite of ice cream, hoping it would calm her. He was about as emotionally committed to her as he was to a ham sandwich. "I'm just telling you, you aren't as perfect as you think you are."

"I never said I was perfect."

She rolled her eyes and took another bite of ice cream, still waiting for it to work its magic. "There are a lot of reasons a woman would not want to be with you. The publicity angle, you never think you're wrong, you are blunt to a fault, you think the world revolves around you, work always comes first, you put in atrocious hours, and you don't believe in love." She pointed her spoon at him. "That, my friend, is reason enough."

"And yet you still wanted to be with me." He crossed the room, leaning on the granite counter.

"Yes, well, I'm in love with you. And I'm stupid enough to actually find some of those things attractive." Another bite of ice cream and still nothing. She dug her spoon deeper into the container.

"But not enough to actually stay with me." His gaze bored holes in her. That must be why he always got what he wanted in negotiations. It was darned unnerving.

"If I give in, you would never love me. You'd think what you signed up for was enough to appease me. I agreed thinking I could coax more out of you, but you'd never love a woman who settled for what you were offering me." She filled her mouth with more ice cream, barely tasting it.

"So you left me to make me love you?" He threw his hands in the air. "You are such a child! I gave you everything you ever wanted, the entire damned Cinderella fantasy!"

"Not even close." She ground the spoon against the side, picking up a glob of fudge.

"You had everything! You should have taken a look in the mirror, because you were completely transformed into a princess. Except the part of Cinderella you wanted wasn't the happily ever after, it was running away and leaving your shoes."

Again with the shoes. "Cinderella was not about how she looked. It was about the prince recognizing the person inside, no matter how she appeared on the outside. It was about love transcending rank and class."

"I thought up the plan when you were wearing one of your awful boxy black suits. It wasn't about how you looked."

"So much for always saying the right thing." She jammed

another spoonful in her mouth, almost a third of the way through the carton.

"You know I didn't mean it like that."

"Listen. I'm tired of fighting with you. Nothing you say is going to change my mind. When I decide to be with someone, it will be a man who loves me so much he can't see straight. And because I love you, Curtis, I want you to feel like that for someone someday, even if it isn't me." She shoveled another spoon of ice cream into her mouth.

Sharp pain began behind her eye, seeping through her brain. She clutched her head, trying not to scream. His warm body was around hers in an instant, trying to pull her hand away.

"What is it?" he begged frantically. "What's happening?"

"I want it to be me," she mumbled, turning into him. The pain eased, releasing as quickly as it came on. "It was just an ice cream headache." She tried to shrug him off, but he held her in his arms, locking her against his bare chest.

He stared down at her, his blue eyes as soft as she'd ever seen them. "I like that about you."

"My intolerance for headaches?"

"That you don't bother with lies."

Oh, that. When he tucked her head beneath his, she gave in, wrapping her arms around him and letting him hold her. Because she'd made love with him tonight and it had been better than her dreams. Because he was so big and safe, while she felt so small and lost. Because his presence was like an opiate, and she was horribly addicted to the way he made her feel. Because she knew soon reality would rush in and she wouldn't be able to.

Curtis prided himself on always knowing how his opponent would respond in a negotiation. He'd never encountered a situation where he had to work with someone so completely irrational they couldn't see reason.

Though his own reasons for wanting to be with her were shifting. He still wanted out of the limelight and knew Heather was the shortest way there, but now he also wanted her. Her kindness, intelligence, and her body pressed so tightly against him he felt singed. He held her tighter, relishing the way she was soft everywhere, not a hard corner anywhere but in her mind.

He was an expert at getting people to see things his way, figuring out what they wanted and giving it to them so they felt obliged to repay his generosity. He hadn't found anything tangible that Heather wanted. The price was too high to give her what she asked for, but there had to be some middle ground. He only needed time to find it.

Time alone with Heather. His groin throbbed at the thought, his body absorbing the heat radiating from her skin. His fingers slid along the ivory silk of her robe, reminding him of how her wedding gown felt. She was a vision in that dress. After she'd run, it hurt him to look at it. The long walk from the yacht to the house he'd had to keep ahead of her so he wouldn't have to see her in it.

"Is this what you would have worn to seduce me?" He slid his hands over her bottom, tracing the lines of the panties she wore beneath the robe.

"I don't know. I doubt it." She tilted her face up so he could take in her bemused grin.

"You didn't have a plan to seduce me, did you?"

"Kind of." She placed her hand on his bare chest. His heart thudded harder, trying to reach her. "I doubted I would have gone through with it. I didn't know what to expect if we were alone."

"I never expected the pool." He returned her smile, then grazed his lips against hers.

"The pool wouldn't have happened. I didn't think you were expecting anything."

"I decided to let you set the pace."

"Then I'd have found the nerve right about never." Her glassy green eyes sparkled with amusement.

"No wonder you ran." Finding the hem of her robe just beneath the curve of her rear, he slid his hands beneath the fabric, only to find another layer. "You thought being with me would be celibate torture." He squeezed her butt, pulling her towards him as he pressed his growing erection against her.

He captured her mouth before she could respond, savoring the coffee and caramel and chocolate. Fantastic. If only he could convince her that her taste in men was as good as her choice in ice cream.

"Let me show you what it would be like, what we would be like." She turned her shoulder to pull away, but he held her firm.

She closed her eyes and shook her head. "We did that in the pool."

"The pool was nothing."

Her head whipped around, her green eyes flashing. "I rocked your world! I—"

His hands on her hips, he lifted her up onto the countertop. Taking advantage of her surprise, he angled his body between her legs.

"The pool was phenomenal, but imagine what we'd be like once we knew each other, knew where to touch." He slid his hands up her pale thighs, pushing the delicate fabric with him. Her whoosh of breath told him he'd found the right place. "Knew where to kiss." Tugging the side of her robe, he brushed it from her shoulder, pressing his lips along the line of her collarbone, trailing kisses up her neck, to the spot just behind her earlobe.

"Sex isn't enough," she said on a breath, not pulling away.

"I don't want to debate, Heather." He pulled back enough to slide her robe from her shoulders, toying with the spaghetti straps of the matching short chemise she wore beneath it. "Let's test the waters, see what we are like together." Deciding he wanted to see her, all of her, he reached for the hem of the lingerie and tried to lift it up.

Heather put her hands down on top of his, stopping him. "We're fantastic together. It clouds the issue."

He shook his head. "No issues. Just step away from reality." He moved his fingers beneath the hem, pulling the back of it from beneath her. "We could knock out every item on your list. Starting with the kitchen." He lifted the chemise above her hips, staring down at pink panties, the words *kiss me* embroidered on the front. His cock swelled at the invitation.

"We can't," she said without effect.

Hooking his thumbs into the side of her panties, he tugged hard, not surprised when she lifted up to help him. "What can't we do?"

"Kiss under a waterfall. See a volcano erupt."

"We'll go to Hawaii on Wednesday." He shrugged off his shirt and rid himself of his pants.

Her giggle went straight through him, his sensations settling in his groin. The skin tightened around his growing erection. He reached for the hem of the chemise. Her hands caught him again.

"There are a lot of lights on in here."

"I know," he groaned, his gaze hungry for more of her naked body.

"Too many lights."

"Making love with the lights on should be on your list."

"It's not."

"Then it is the first entry on mine."

"But I don't look like—" He silenced her insecurities with a kiss he hoped would burn out the last vestiges of doubt in her mind that he was thinking of anyone else. He didn't want mechanical sex, he wanted Heather alive and vibrant. He wanted to drown in her, to bury himself so deep some of her kindness and enthusiasm rubbed off.

When he pulled back to remove the chemise from her, the eager, expectant look in her eye clenched his gut. She had a way of looking at him in a way he'd never experienced. He liked it, but if he took the time to think about why, too many things would have to change.

The chemise joined the rest of their clothes on the kitchen floor. Heather wrapped her arms around his neck, pulling him closer.

"I wasn't going to sleep with you again."

"Glad I could talk you out of that." He pulled her flush against him, his fingers twitching on her hips. With her hot wetness slick against him, he fought the primal urge to take her now, without any warning, but he couldn't give in. That would be too easy. He'd never been this out of control with need, lust, and he liked the high it gave him. The thrill of skating on sharp edges at midnight, not caring where you were going, only how fast you could go.

Lowering his head, he took her mouth, kissing her with all

the determination he could muster. He fisted one hand in her hair, anchoring her to him, tipping her head back and exposing her throat. He trailed the kiss across her jaw, to the place at the base of her throat where her pulse beat fast and thready beneath her skin.

He needed her like he needed to breathe. He didn't know why, had spent so long distancing himself from any feeling, anything that could be lost and not regained, that he doubted love was possible for him. It required a depth of emotion he never cared to revisit. Yet, here and now, he felt something that couldn't be written off as base carnal desire. Absolute freedom was as close as he could come to describing it. He wanted more, and he never wanted it to end.

"I don't understand you," he said on a groan, his hands roving her body while his eyes feasted on the aroused blush of her bare skin.

"I know." Soft fingers glided down his shoulders, chest, circled his belly button. "And I understand you completely. More so now than ever." She reached between them, her slim fingers wrapping around his length.

The taut pink nipples of her breasts were his best hope at distraction. He traced slow circles around her areolas, amazed when Heather matched his pace with her hand. Releasing one breast, he licked his thumb, then pulled her ripe nipple between two fingers, twitching the sensitive nub with his thumb. Her breath hitched, her eyelids lowering seductively. When he did the same to the other breast, her pace faltered, but just as quickly she took her bottom lip between her teeth and started to stroke him in earnest.

His entire world shrunk, sensations multiplying until he could feel every brush of her fingers all the way up his spine. So much for wanting to take it slow. He could feel the tightening of his muscles starting, clenching for the promised release.

"Enough," he growled into a kiss, pulling her hand away and placing it on the counter. "I don't know what it is, but I need to be inside you. Now."

With his free hand he opened her to him, sliding all the way in with one swift stroke. He kissed her mouth, plundering and taking with the same passion as he thrust into her. A blind rush, a mad frenzy, an exhilarating high.

She broke the kiss, her lips trailing to his ear as he leaned closer, racing with his own pleasure. Her teeth tugged at his earlobe before she whispered, "It's what you were afraid of."

His confusion was lost as her orgasm hit hard, her fingers digging into his shoulders, the aroused blush flushing bright pink across her neck and chest. Her tight walls seized, pulsing and tightening in a way he couldn't resist.

Through clenched teeth, his raw groan echoed through the house, promising the other rooms they'd soon get their turn.

"What am I afraid of?"

Heather blinked, surprised to find Curtis in her room. After their lovemaking in the kitchen she'd said she was tired and needed a shower, but he made no offer to go with her. Yet here he was, catching her with wet hair, barely clothed, and unable to see clearly. The déjà vu of the moment wasn't lost, but this time she wouldn't promise anything she wasn't getting in return. She cinched the towel tighter across her breasts, modesty still prevailing though he'd seen every inch of her.

"Earlier, I said I didn't know what was happening and you said it was what I was afraid of. What is that supposed to mean?" His nostrils flared as he stared at her, arms crossed over his broad chest, now covered in a maroon t-shirt.

She stepped closer, knowing she was overplaying her hand, but she had nothing more to lose. She'd left her pride with her shoes on the church steps. She only wanted him if she could have all of him, and he wasn't about to let her go because he so hated to lose.

"You have something to lose now, besides your one-way ticket off the paparazzi stalking list."

"Excuse me?" He stepped back, bumping into the wall.

"You said if I wanted love, we'd make it. So we did. And you are afraid of losing that, of losing me."

"Heather, you're setting yourself up for disappointment again." He uncrossed his arms, leaning back against the wall. "I'm not wired to fall in love the way you want me to. We have so many other things, stronger things going for us."

"Is that why you picked me? Because I am the easiest for you to get along with? How far down your list of bridal choices was I?" Panic flooded her veins, making her want to run outside and swim to shore. Anything to get away from her deluded reality.

"You were my only choice."

"And why do you think that was?" She tried to think up some snarky, nasty put-down to make him feel as low as he made her, but instead of speaking he crossed the room in two steps. He framed her face in his hands, pressing his lips against hers in a bruising kiss. It was all she could do to place a hand on his chest and push, turning her head.

"No, Curtis." She shook her head, the cool ends of her damp hair taunting her heated skin. "You won't share my bed again until you can open yourself up to loving me."

His hands dropped to her bare arms, burning into her flesh as he squeezed. "I want you and I need you. It's enough."

"It's as good as sitting on a two-legged barstool. Chemistry and compatibility won't weather any storms. I don't want to be your first wife, Curtis. I want to be your last, your only."

He dropped his hands and her throat tightened, her eyes growing heavy with unshed tears.

"Every day since we met my soul has reached out for yours, and each time you turn your back. Standing in the church this morning I realized, you wanted it to stay the same forever. If I had allowed things to continue, you would never have realized you love me. You wouldn't have to."

"Heather, it's not you. I can't—"

She held up a hand, exhausted by his constant protests. "You can, and you do. That's why I was the only one you thought of, why you brought me here, why we're drawn together like the moon and the tide. But until you want to, we're both in for a world of hurt."

"You have some fairy tale notion of what love is. What can love give you that I can't?"

"Trust." The word came automatically, but hearing it she knew it was right. "You'll be attracted to other women, others will make themselves indispensable to you. I need to know there is a reason you come home every night, a reason you sleep alone when you are traveling." She pressed her shaking hands into the terry cloth of the towel, her stomach clenching.

His head shook, his jaw twitching. "I have never done *anything* to make you question my loyalty."

"You claim to have chosen a bride on paper. What's to keep you from opting for someone more compatible?"

"We have a contract. I honor my dealings, you know that."

"And where in your precious contract was fucking on the kitchen counter?" Her voice rose with every syllable.

His mouth opened, his eyes widening. About time she'd rendered him speechless. They had equal roles in how things fell apart, but now Heather decided to be honest with herself. Maybe he would be too, but she was no longer going to hope for it as she had before.

She cleared her throat, fiddling with the hem of the towel. "Look. No one wants us to work out more than me. But the us I want, the one I agreed to when I signed the contract, doesn't only exist on paper, in the bedroom or in the office. It's bigger than that. And unless that is what you want too, there is no point in even negotiating. I'm firm on my terms. I won't be with a man who doesn't love me."

Chapter Ten

The subtle sweetness of summer blew in off the lake as Curtis ran around the perimeter of the island. He tried to focus on the bright morning sun, the clear blue sky, the verdant clusters of trees on the hills that sloped into the lake.

He hadn't expected to like it here, on this sapphire lake, in a house last decorated the year he was born, but in spite of fighting with Heather, he wanted to stay. Away from the questions, where he could get some perspective on the situation.

He'd felt like a total cad last night, leaving her crying in her room, but she didn't want him to comfort her. She wanted him to love her, and since he couldn't, she wanted nothing to do with him. Not now, not when they got back to the city, not ever.

He'd had a few deals sour, and always found a way to come out better for it in the end, but he couldn't let this one go. He knew he should be cutting his losses, taking her back to her parents, and leaving her to wallow in the mess she'd made. He'd considered it last night, all night since he couldn't sleep for dreaming about her. He didn't like the finality of it.

He didn't understand anything he felt right now. He wasn't reacting normally, logically. He should have fed her to the paparazzi and been done with her, instead of protecting her and whisking her away here. He should have admonished her for the embarrassment and scandal she caused, not order Kendra to keep it at bay. He shouldn't want to see her at all, and yet he'd gone on a run to keep from waking her.

Rounding the south side of the island, his feet pounded the ruddy ground. He looked up to see the back elevation of the house, trees he hadn't bothered to notice last night blocking the view of the pool. He grinned, the memory snapshots in his mind. They had something, and it wasn't all she wanted it to be, but it was close.

Close enough for a compromise. Surely she'd be open to that. He picked up his pace, running for the house.

Streams of light filtered through the windows, too bright for her eyes to take in without squinting. The pleasures she'd indulged in last night left her body with the dull ache of exertion. She stretched her arms overhead, yawning deep. Until she caught the scent of Curtis in the room.

She turned over, sitting up against the pillows and pulling the blankets with her. Sure enough, he sat in the chair next to the vanity, eyeing her over his PDA.

"What are you doing in here?" The throaty sound of her voice gave the words a subtext of invitation, so she cleared her throat.

He held up the device. "Checking my email. The new assistant sends me every single one. Such a waste of my time." He laid the device on the vanity, next to a plate of croissants and her glasses. She slid them on instantly. He must have kept them when he took them off her in the church yesterday.

"New assistant?" She'd expected to be fired, but not replaced so quickly.

"From the same agency you worked for. I don't know why she's so overwhelmed, she barely has to do anything."

"Being your assistant is a big job—"

"I'm not even there." He ran his hand through his hair, sending the short-cropped pieces into disarray. "There can't be that much to do when I'm not around?"

"Yes, there is." His eyes widened and her heart softened. Here was a problem she knew how to solve. "Can you get me a phone?"

"Why?"

"A phone, that PDA, and the croissants. I'll have this fixed for you by the time you get back up here with orange juice and coffee."

Curtis crossed the room, his brow furrowing. He set the plate and PDA on the bedside table, eyeing her suspiciously as he left the room. When he returned a minute later with the phone she was halfway through an almond croissant and had found the phone numbers she needed.

Instead of getting her juice, he sat and stared as she made the necessary calls, sliding an employee from Golden City's administrative pool into an assistant position for one of the semi-retired partners and snagging that assistant for Curtis. She briefed the new assistant on where she kept the position manual she'd written, as well as what to look out for while Curtis was away.

She clicked off the phone, brushing the crumbs from the blanket. "My juice?"

He tilted his head to the side, eyes narrowing. "You wrote a position manual?"

"I was gearing up to ask you for a raise, and since you don't know what I do—did—I thought it would help my case. Now that I'm fired, it will save the next person from your wrath."

"I didn't fire you."

Yeah, right. "I have a job to go back to next Monday?"

"Being my assistant is no longer appropriate." He brushed imaginary crumbs from his burgundy t-shirt, *Stanford* printed across his chest.

"So I'm fired." Why was it he never wanted to say the words? The man danced around everything with the grace of Fred Astaire.

Heather pushed off the blankets and climbed out of bed, the pink satin nightgown she wore nearly touching the floor. It would be modest, if the slit on her hip didn't go clear past her panties.

Snagging the empty plate, she started towards the door. Warm fingers wrapped around her arm, stalling her progress.

"Where are you going?"

"To get some juice." The man's touch sent quivers straight to her spine. She stared down at his fingers, sighing in relief when he removed them. "And scan the internet for jobs, now that I am unemployed."

"You don't need a job." He followed her down the stairs.

"Tell that to my landlord." She froze, grasping the railing for support. She didn't have a place to live. Her lease had expired and her roommates had found a place without her. All of her things had been moved to Curtis's house last week. She'd set everything up in a spare room Mrs. Rutledge claimed was never used.

Heather, honey. You really didn't think this running-away thing through.

Shaking her head, she slowly made it down the stairs. She hadn't thought at all, just felt and ran. Maybe there was something to be said for Curtis's logic-over-emotion way of life. If she'd followed his rules, she would have ended up with a severance package and letter of recommendation. Her way she was homeless, jobless, and on the run from the paparazzi. Maybe she needed to think more and feel less.

She made her way into the kitchen, shocked to find the dishes she'd left soaking in the sink last night cleaned and dried, sitting on the counter.

"You did the dishes?"

His shoulders bunched in an exasperated shrug. "It's ten in the morning. I had to do something while you slept the day away."

"I was exhausted." She still felt the heaviness of her actions on her shoulders. Maybe she should crawl back into bed and pull the covers up over her head.

"You should go for a run or have a swim."

Heather placed a hand on her rounded stomach, another against her full hip. Did he think she was tired because she was overweight and couldn't keep up with him?

"I'm emotionally exhausted, Curtis." Pulling open a cupboard, she plucked out a glass and set it on the counter so hard it clanged.

"I figured. Exercise will clear your head, put things in perspective."

Her stomach fluttered, recalling the perspective her last swim had given her. She pulled open the refrigerator and snagged the orange juice. Finally, she poured herself a glass and drank it down.

"Thirsty?" Curtis chuckled as she poured another.

"Someone didn't bring me anything to drink."

"You didn't say please."

"I didn't think it was in your vocabulary."

"Why are you so angry at me?" He stepped to her, running his hands up and down her bare arms as the skin came alive. "I can feel the tension coming off you."

"We did not end the evening on good terms." She stared up at him, trying to convince herself to step back, get distance. But her brain was the only part of her that didn't want to fall against him and beg him to make all this mess go away. "And yet I woke up to find you in my room."

"I was hoping a good night's rest would give you a different outlook."

Of course he wouldn't give up so easy. "Your new assistant is male, so you'll have to look elsewhere for your bridal selection process."

His fingers tightened on her arms, his light eyes glaring at her. "I will be with you, or I will be with no one. Your choice. That is the last we talk about it on this island. We have a wonderful opportunity here. For us to get to know each other, to do a trial run of the relationship so you can be completely sure it isn't enough for you, and to plan the redesign of this house."

Stunned into silence, she could only nod. If he wanted her, or no one, that had to mean something. Maybe she wasn't as delusional as she thought.

"Then we're agreed. I found something for you." He took her hand, pulling her out of the kitchen and towards the stairs.

"Are you sure you still want me working on the plans? Since I'm not a Golden employee?"

"Golden doesn't own Sapphire Isle, I do." At the second floor landing he kept going, climbing the next flight.

At the top of the stairs he led her past the library and game room, pulling her down the hallway. She knew exactly where they were going and froze, pulling her hand from his.

"I didn't change my mind about sleeping with you." Even in the master suite, with the panoramic view of the lake, tempting as it might be.

"I had nothing to do with this." His hand moved to reach for hers, but he pulled it back. He turned, opening the door to the master suite.

Hesitantly, Heather followed behind him. She'd thought of making over the suite before they arrived, but left it off as too expensive. The bathroom alone was the size of her apartment in San Francisco. Scratch that, former apartment.

The dark green carpet and wood-paneled walls dated the room, as did the giant shiny brass bed. With a facelift it would be breathtaking, but until then, the bathroom with the redwood sauna, double shower, and sunken marble tub was the best asset of the room.

"Through here," Curtis called, walking through the bathroom as if it weren't a work of art.

Down the hall lay the long-empty dressing rooms she planned to convert into another bedroom. But past the doors her world tilted. The room was filled with clothes. Wooden hangers hung from every bar, shoes lined the floor.

"What is this?" She turned around, taking it all in. She didn't see individual pieces, the swirl of color shocking her. Rusty oranges and warm browns, smooth creams and pops of bright green and pale pink spun as she twirled.

"This is Dahlia Frye at her best. She left a card."

Heather stopped to take the envelope, guilt niggling at her. The troubling feeling deepened as she read the card.

Welcome to our family, Heather. We are all so pleased our

Curtis has found someone so utterly devoted to him. Since we both know his aversion to black, I thought it might be nice to give you some more colorful options.

"You hate black?"

"Despise it."

And that was all she ever wore. "Why didn't you say something?"

"I have two sisters. I know better than to tell a woman what to wear." He grinned from ear to ear. "Besides, that's my mother's job."

She looked wistfully around the room, then down at her nightgown. "I can't accept this."

Curtis rolled his eyes, pulling open a drawer of belts. "Try the life on for the rest of the week. All of it."

His gaze caught hers with a wicked, suggestive gleam. Hope danced across her heart. If he wanted her this badly, he had to feel something. He might be as expressive as a brick wall, but maybe he was as afraid of losing what they could be as she was.

Part of her scoffed at the notion as she wrestled with her conscience. What would it hurt to try on the life? At least parts of it. She reached out, her fingers tickling along a pink sundress.

"Go ahead, try it on."

She lifted the hanger from the rod, holding the dress against her body. "Okay. Give me a minute to change."

He shook his head, slow and purposeful. "I want to watch."

Her heart pounded in her chest, the devil on her shoulder telling her to go for it, but she'd made a decision and she had to stand by it. She tilted up her chin, plastering on a façade of boldness. "I don't think so. Why don't you wait in the other room?"

His ominous frown made him look surprised, as if he expected a closet full of clothes to pull him back into her good graces. “You don’t like the new wardrobe?”

“Did you think new outfits would make me want to sleep with you?”

The way his head snapped back in alarm gave her some relief. At least he understood he’d been insulting, even if he hadn’t realized it before.

“I’m not ready to try the whole life on. But I’m willing to start with the clothes.”

With a sharp nod he retreated from the room without so much as a backwards glance. Heather sighed, unsure what she wanted from him, from herself. Everything was such a jumble, taking the next few days off to relax and explore the limited possibilities with Curtis tempted her. She was already in love with him, what was she protecting herself from, really?

With a wistful smile she shed the nightgown, slipping into the pink, ruffle-trimmed sundress. She couldn’t quite get the zipper in the back, and instead of contorting herself she walked into the bedroom. Curtis sat in a brown leather armchair, staring at the horizon.

“Can you zip me up?” She turned so her back was to him and swept her hair over her shoulder. His knuckles grazed her skin as he pulled the zipper. Leather crunched when he sat back down.

“Turn around.”

She performed a teasing pirouette, running her hands over the delicate material.

“I like it.”

She looked down to where he sat, watching his gaze pour over her like a physical touch. When his gaze met hers, his warm, mischievous grin caused her to raise an eyebrow.

"Me too." She turned her back to him, pulling her hair aside again. "Now unzip me so I can try on something else."

Strutting like a model on a runway, she paraded a dozen outfits past him. Skirts and sweaters, pants and cardigans, jeans and jackets. Enthusiasm sparkled in her eyes.

Out she came, in a ruffled tuxedo shirt and slacks that made her legs look miles long. Gorgeous, except for the look on her face.

"Did you tell your mother you were firing me?"

He shook his head, wary of the glint in her eye. "I didn't fire you."

"There aren't many work clothes. There are only two suits in there."

"And?"

Heather shook her head, marching back into the closet. Curtis shook his head too, wondering if there was any decoder ring for what that woman thought. He was good at reading people, prided himself on it, but she was an enigma.

She'd always been so good at anticipating what he wanted at work, delivering before he even asked, it shocked him she wanted every last detail spelled out now. Especially when all the decisions were hers to make. There were plenty of committees to chair, fundraisers to plan. Hell, she could redecorate the house. She wouldn't be wanting for things to do.

She strode down the hall with purpose, stopping right in front of him in a bold green dress and matching jacket. He blinked at the creamy mounds of her breasts peeking over the top of the strapless dress. Nice.

"This is completely inappropriate for work."

"It's a suit." Not the kind she used to wear, but if she had...

She shrugged off the jacket, tossing it across his lap and placing her hands on her hips. "This is a strapless dress. For work?"

"Maybe she wanted you to dress more your age."

"My age? I need to dress more professionally because I am young, not less. Every man who comes into the office for a meeting will be staring at my boobs."

She had him there. He tore his gaze away. "You don't have to like everything she picks out."

Her chest rose and fell as she huffed. "She knew I didn't have a job, and I didn't."

"I didn't tell her, she assumed. It would be awkward for us to work together now."

"Yes, now. But not if everything had worked out."

He leveled his gaze at her. "I'm not asking you to get my coffee and sort my mail."

"Then when would I see you? You live at the office."

"At home, after work."

"At night, for sex." She shook her head, returning to the closet.

When she put it like that, it sounded awful. But it also meant she'd have the freedom and money to be completely independent. Why did she have to always see things negatively? He'd thought this would cheer her up, and it only seemed to make things worse.

There had to be something he could do to calm her, make her see what a great life she could have if she'd just look beyond her Cinderella fairy tale. He wished he knew what to say to get her to see things from his side.

"You have got to be kidding me," Heather called out.

"What is it?" Curtis stood, unsure if going into the closet would get him screamed at, or worse, start her crying again.

"Your mother thinks I'm a slut."

"No she doesn't." Dahlia preferred the term *loose*, and had liberally applied it to women he'd been reported to be dating. She'd been completely in favor of Heather. *Such a nice girl.*

"This says she does." Heather marched through the doors, clad in jeans and a creamy lace camisole laced up the front, the satin ribbons playing peek-a-boo with her naked flesh beneath.

His mouth watered and he swallowed, twice. "You look fantastic."

"Where am I going to wear a shirt that laces up the front?" She placed her hands on her hips, stretching the patience of the ribbon and his.

"Home." He stepped to her, reaching out to undo the tiny bow she'd tied. She caught his hand.

"What do you think you're doing?"

"Helping you undress?"

"I've got it, thanks." She took a step back. "You know, you need to try on the life too. It won't be a non-stop naked party."

He exaggerated a pout. "Why not?"

She smiled, that big fake smile she gave delivery people. "You want a whore, hire one." She turned on her heel and marched back through the doors.

Who knew nice Heather Tindall had such a mean side? He doubted there was a person who knew her who'd believe how nasty she was being. It's not like he'd picked out the clothes, and she enjoyed herself as much as he did when they were naked.

Curtis marched through the bathroom, back to the closet, then knocked on the partly closed door. "Heather?"

Something clunked against the wall, making him step back and reevaluate. Would she really throw something at him?

"I don't like how this is going."

"Me either," she said from inside.

"I thought this would make you happy, not having to wear lingerie all the time. I thought—"

She stepped through the doorway, still in the jeans, but she'd changed to a crocheted tank the same pale green as the middle of her eyes. Her brows knit together, her teeth worrying her luscious bottom lip. He hardened, remembering how he'd feasted on her succulent mouth.

Her angry scowl eased. "I overreacted. I know it's not what you meant."

He nodded, trying to tread carefully.

"I think I overreact because you don't react at all."

He raised an eyebrow. "I'm having a reaction."

She rolled her eyes. "You're getting turned on because of the cleavage factor."

"That *is* a reaction."

"Not the one I want." Her lower lip trembled, quickening his pulse. He hated nothing more than being the cause of her tears.

"I loved it the first time Dahlia picked out a wardrobe for me. It felt amazingly freeing to get out of the black and have everything be new. I wanted you to have that feeling too."

Her face relaxed, her eyes widening in a smile as she leaned against the doorframe. "How old were you when the Fryes adopted you?"

"Nine." He hadn't meant to open himself up for a question-and-answer session.

"Why did you wear black?"

"He decided we both needed to stay in mourning after my mother died." Curtis never knew what to call the man who'd chosen revenge over his son. Father didn't fit anymore.

"Why did you change your name?"

"Because Jason Frye is ten years older than me, and Jason Curtis murdered someone. It was another fresh start."

"Mrs. Rutledge still calls you Jason."

He nodded. "She's known me since before the Fryes. She was the one who asked them to take me in."

"You're very lucky to have her."

"She lived next door. She and my mother used to talk after work while I played in her yard because it was bigger than ours. I think after the accident she wanted to make sure I was okay, out of duty to my mother. She always told me my father would pull out of his obsession with vengeance, but she didn't know about the drugs." The words poured out of his mouth like rain from a thunderhead. He'd said more than he planned, but he didn't know how to get the water back into the cloud.

Heather reached out, wrapping her small, soft hand around his. "Thank you for trying to give me the feeling you had." She squeezed his hand, stepping out of the doorway to stand next to him. "Let's get to work on the plans for the house. I don't want to leave this project unfinished."

She released his hand, walking past him and then out of the suite. He followed, amazed she hadn't pried for more, hadn't grilled him the way others did when he didn't give them half the opening.

He stood taller, proud of having told her. He never did because of the way people reacted, but she hadn't reacted at all. There hadn't been a shred of pity in her eyes.

Calm washed over him as he left the room. If she could

accept him as he was, damaged past and all, she was more than just the convenient fiancée he'd hoped for. She was a friend and a partner, someone he could trust absolutely. With anything.

Chapter Eleven

"You haven't touched your wine."

Heather stared at the deep red liquid in the glass, wondering if she dared. When she drank, the tiny part of her still in control of her responses to him was silenced. Leaving her to do some thoughtless things, like agree to this charade in the first place, and seduce him in a swimming pool.

"Are you feeling all right?"

"I'm fine." She forced a smile, trying to keep her mind from wandering to what would happen after dinner. Stabbing her fork at a few more vodka-sauce-drenched penne, she continued to eat. The pasta was warm and comforting, exactly what she needed now when temptation loomed large.

He'd been so sweet today, especially after the way she'd overreacted to the clothes. She'd thought agreeing to pose as his fiancée would mean more time together, not less. Everyone seemed to catch that little snag in her plan, except her. She hadn't seen anything, except a way to get what she wanted, however unrealistic.

They were both guilty of the same thing, wanting their own perfect and not thinking the other person would have a completely different version. Surprisingly, their minds were in agreement about what to do with Sapphire Isle. He took in every suggestion she made, accepting it with an explanation as to why. Working with him today had been like taking a hands-on master's course in property development.

He'd shown her things she hadn't thought of, like the security headquarters and the places the island was approachable by boats. She'd been on the lookout for cameras, wondering if they were being watched from the forest surrounding the lake, but saw no one.

"Did you see any paparazzi when we were out today?"

He shook his head. "Did you?"

"No. I was wondering why they seem to be leaving us alone."

"Oh. Kendra emailed that a pop tart had a quickie Vegas wedding the same day as your tantrum." He raised his glass. "To unexpected deflections."

Tantrum indeed. "To sudden realizations." She lifted her glass in a toast, then tasted the warm richness of the full-bodied red wine. The flavors rolled over her tongue, heating her mouth and loosening her mind.

"It will probably pick back up again when we return home. But it fizzles after a while and we'll be left to ourselves." Curtis finished his plate, tearing into a buttered roll.

"What will we tell them?"

"The press? Whatever you decide, I suppose. We could say we're moving slower so you can get used to the media attention, and will marry when it dies down."

"We're not engaged anymore, contractually or otherwise." The words exhaled on a breath.

"Then we'll stick with your cold feet."

She cleared her throat. "Are you not hearing me, or just not taking no as an answer?"

"Heather, we agreed not to talk about this now. We're going

to take the next few days to try on the life, see how it feels so you can make an informed decision. I've accepted you want more than a business relationship, welcomed it. Why can't you keep an open mind as well?"

No matter what he gave her, showed her, nothing could convince her to marry a man who wasn't in love with her. She didn't want a first husband, she wanted a husband. Period. No disclaimers.

"Ice cream for dessert?" Curtis stood, taking his plate and hers.

"I can do that." She set her napkin on the table, starting to get up.

"You don't have to. You made dinner, I can put the dishes in the sink." He strode confidently back into the house.

Guilt tickled at her. She hadn't made dinner, exactly. Just warmed up the meal her roommates had prepared, the same way she'd done at lunch. They might live together technically, but they'd never spent a night under the same roof until they came here. And at home, they had a housekeeper who was brilliant in the kitchen.

"I can't cook," she said as soon as Curtis returned to the veranda with a pint of ice cream and two spoons.

"Okay." He sat in the chair opposite her and handed her a spoon.

"You said I made dinner and I didn't." Saying the words loosened her nerves.

"So there are elves around here who cook?" He dug into the pint, coming up with a pink and white swirled spoonful.

"No. My roommates made the food. I just heat it up."

"And that's not cooking?" The spoon disappeared between his lips.

"No, that's reheating." She stared at the pint, trying to make out the flavor.

"You're honest to a fault, aren't you?"

"Saves time." She clutched her spoon, wondering how to get the pint away from him.

"And yet you let people think our engagement was as real as you wanted it to be." Again with the spoon. Really, this was a cruel form of torture.

"I thought it was. Or would be, eventually."

"So at the church, what happened?"

"A wake-up call from my delusions." She met his gaze. "I don't want to talk about this anymore, and I want the ice cream."

He took another spoonful, then handed it over. "It's interesting to me."

"I'll bet." Creamy cheesecake and sweet strawberries filled her mouth. Good choice.

"You feel everything so deeply. The slightest thing can affect you. Was it always that way?"

"I guess." She shifted in her seat, staring out at where the sun had recently left the horizon. The oranges and pinks of the sunset quickly turning to blues and purples. He reached his spoon across the table, stealing a bite.

"I don't think of things the way you do. I do what feels right instead of what looks right on paper." She shoved a spoonful into her mouth to keep from saying too much.

She studied his face as his features changed from interested to completely unreadable. Anyone else would have thought he couldn't care less. But Heather had been learning him for months, and the blank expression meant one of two things. Either he was bored, or he was worried.

She stared harder in the silence, wondering why he would worry, and then it hit her. He didn't believe she was in love with him, but if he realized she was always honest, he had to also realize she told the truth about her feelings. She took an accomplished bite of the ice cream, letting it melt slowly over her tongue.

He cleared his throat. "In business, and in the social circles, it is important to be able to play a kind of game, telling people what they want to hear. Can you do that?" He snatched the carton from her hand, digging in.

"No. But I don't think you need to. Life runs a lot smoother when you are straight with people and not always having to decipher what they mean from what they say."

"I don't think it would work." He raised his spoon to silence her when she began to protest. "But I'm willing to give it a shot. I think you should be the project manager on the Sapphire Isle venture."

Her mouth opened in surprise. Jumping up and kissing him for his faith in her and the opportunity came to her mind first, but the possibility of sinister motives behind his action kept her seated.

"Why me?" She tugged the nearly empty carton back from him.

"You've done the work. Your reports are complete, your ideas solid. And you said you wanted to keep working. You could manage this project, then find another for yourself after that. Or work in party planning like you wanted to before coming to work for me."

"So it's not working you're against, just working with you all the time." She took a huge bite, letting the coldness chill her ire.

"You're no longer in a position to be my assistant, Heather.

Why can't you see that?" He took back the carton, scraping his spoon against the bottom to finish it.

"I can. I just thought we would talk about it, instead of you steamrolling over me."

"You act like I force you into things. That's not fair."

She met his gaze, knowing they each had a point. "You're right, you don't force me, but you assume I want what you want without asking."

"Do you want to manage the Sapphire Isle project?"

"Yes."

"Then why are we arguing, exactly?" He lifted a brow in a flirtatious challenge.

"Because you finished the ice cream."

"There's more, but really, I think there are better things we could be doing." He stood from the table, plucking the spoon from her hand.

"I'm still not having sex with you." Her stomach tightened. If he pushed, she'd relent. Sex was the only way he was willing to connect with her, and she didn't want to lose that. But more so, she didn't want to lose herself.

"You agreed to try on the life. Sharing my bed is part of that." Grabbing her hand, he tugged her up against him.

"I think it's time *you* try on the life, Curtis. We won't make love constantly."

"Why not?" He had the nerve to grin.

"Because people get sick, and tired, and a whole host of other reasons. I'll share a bed with you, but only to sleep."

"Can you do that?"

✧

Curtis clutched the book in his hand, staring down at the ridiculous silk boxers Heather had given him from her pink suitcase when he told her he slept in the nude. That bridal shower had gotten them both in trouble. Heather had a case full of lingerie that made her uncomfortable, and he was stuck with boxers that simply were uncomfortable. *Boxer shorts don't even have a purpose.*

He knocked softly on the semi-closed door, then pushed it open, finding Heather sitting up against the pillows in the bronze bed, her long brown hair draped over her shoulders, almost hiding the lacy pink nightgown she wore. The lamp on her bedside table gave a soft glow, the light blocked in by the curtains hanging from the bed crown, illuminated as if only the bed existed in the entire room.

She smiled at him, closing the book he only just now realized she held. He stepped into the room, more nervous than he'd been in a decade. Even yesterday in the church he hadn't been anxious, until she ran.

"*Great Expectations*?"

"Not exactly." It took him a moment to realize she meant the book. He held it up. "*The Mayor of Casterbridge.*"

Her grin widened, her eyes sparkling. She held up her book. "*Return of the Native.*"

He shook his head, making his way to the side of the bed. "I'm surprised. I had you pegged for happy endings."

"It's a happy ending for Tomasin."

"Just barely."

She shrugged her shoulders and pulled back the coverlet next to her, not letting an inch of her nightgown show. That had to be difficult in the queen bed. "What did you think I'd be reading?"

"Bronte. Austen. Eliot. There isn't anything from this century or last in the library, or I'd have pegged you for a romance reader." He sat next to her, still keeping his feet on the floor.

"Any of those and I would have stayed up all night reading. Hardy has better chapter breaks. Why *Mayor of Casterbridge*? Are you worried your past is going to come back to haunt you?"

It already had. "I couldn't find *Great Expectations*."

She grinned, turning to take a book from her bedside table. She handed him *Great Expectations*. "I wasn't sure if you'd go through with this experiment, and if you did, I thought you might need something to distract yourself with."

"Besides you." He'd had the same thought, which was why he'd stopped in the library for a book.

"Exactly."

"Aren't we a little young to be reading in bed, when there are so many more stimulating things to do?" Her skin took on a honeyed hue in the lamplight. Why had he ever thought Heather Tindall was the easy way out? She was full of surprises, and rules, and temptation. He'd never seen it coming.

"Reading seems to be something we actually have in common. When did you start reading the classics?"

"I don't know if they are classics, or just old books. But my mother taught English literature at a private school—she had the house stocked with books by dead people."

"Dahlia was a teacher? I thought she was a designer."

He shook his head, opening the book and leaning back against the pillows piled against the headboard. "Not Dahlia. The Fryes have a library at their estate too. I kept reading once I got there."

Warm fingers rested on his arm, and he didn't really want

them there. He didn't want to shake her off, but he didn't want her pity either. So a reckless driver killed his mother, so his world spun out of control when his father couldn't handle the loss. It didn't matter. He was lucky to have been taken in by a family who gave him every opportunity to succeed.

The weight of her stare pulled at him to turn his head, but he wasn't going down that road again. She didn't need a tour of his damaged psyche to make her decision, just a night in a bed where he kept his hands off her. Easily done in this mood.

He sat stiffly once her attention was back on her book, his mind running too fast to slow down and make sense of the pages in front of him. Sitting in bed with her was too intimate, almost more personal than making love with her. That had a purpose, a beginning and an end. This was as ridiculous as the silk boxer shorts sliding against him.

With a clap, her book closed and she set it on the nightstand beside her. "Could you turn your lamp on if you want to keep reading? I'm going to go to sleep."

"Sleep sounds good." Once she was asleep he could sneak out of here, take off the damned shorts, and get some rest. He closed his book, watching as she fluffed her pillows, then switched off the light.

In a few moments his eyes had adjusted to the moonlight illuminating the edges of objects in the room. Heather lay on her side, facing him, her hair spilling over the pillow. He wanted to both run from the intimacy of the moment, and drown in it. He didn't have much experience in connecting with other people. Even before the accident, his father had been distant. The Fryes were big on expectation, low on comfort.

Heather was comfort incarnate. Big eyes that warmed you from the inside out, a smile so wide it forced you to smile back, and there was something about her that made everyone fall in love with her instantly.

His chest tightened, his heart pounding wildly against his chest. He couldn't possibly.

"You're staring at me," she said, without opening her eyes.

"I can't do this." He sat up, but her hand on his arm stalled his escape.

"This is important to me, Curtis. Please."

"I wouldn't do this."

She propped up on an elbow. "Do what? Sleep? Even you must sleep."

"Fall asleep without touching you."

"I need you to. If you can't, then you are as blinded by sex as I am by my infatuation with you, and we're really in trouble. You have to be the rational one. You have to do this."

"You want me to try on the life. I wouldn't do this. I wouldn't wear this, I wouldn't sit in bed and read when we could be doing something else, I wouldn't be able to fall asleep knowing you're right there."

"You want me to be waiting to warm your bed when you get home in the middle of the night?"

"I'd leave the office earlier if I had a reason to."

"Oh, you would not." Heather laughed, batting him on the arm. "We need to be honest about what is going on here. I have some crazy notion we can be together, and you are stringing me along because you want out of the spotlight and we happen to be good together in bed."

"We've never been in a bed."

"Is that the problem?" Sarcasm laced her voice.

"No, I doubt I could sleep beside you in the kitchen either." Incredulity at the idea made him chuckle.

"How can we get along so well all day, then at night we can't even sleep together?"

"We were working all day. Now there is just you in bed with me. I can't concentrate." He ran his hands through his hair, surely standing it on end. He smashed it back against his scalp.

"You are really freaking out." Heather got up on her knees, facing him.

"Yeah. Know a church I can run away from?"

She swatted his arm. "It's the island. I'm literally the only woman here. Back in town you'll be fine."

Only if she agreed to stay with him before they made it back to real life. If not, he'd live in this purgatory. "I still wouldn't be able to do this. I can't lie here and not touch you."

"Sure you can."

"No, I can't."

"People don't have sex every single day."

"Why not?" Her lips tilted in a grin. Well, at least they agreed on that.

"What would you do then?"

He stood, shucking off the tormenting silk. "Those are beyond ridiculous." He sat back on the bed, lifting his leg up and under the comforter, then pulling it up to his waist. "Much better."

"Except now you're naked."

"That is how I sleep. You should try it."

"That is *not* how I sleep."

"And you sleep in one of these?" He turned, propping himself on an elbow, facing her as he ran his finger against the rough lacy strap of her nightgown. The whole thing was a stretch peek-a-boo lace that hid nothing. She really should be naked. It would be much more comfortable, and convenient.

"I sleep in pajamas, but no one bought me pajamas. They all thought you'd appreciate this more."

He wrinkled his nose, trying to decide. He'd want her comfortable. "They're wrong."

"I thought so too, but since we never discussed sleeping arrangements, I thought it best to humor them."

"Sleeping arrangements are up to you. Even now, it seems. Though I won't be able to sleep with you unless I can touch you, and restricting sleep is one of the most effective forms of torture."

"Stop pushing me to do what you want."

"We both want." He traced the edge of her jaw with his finger.

"That's what scares me. There is something behind what I feel for you, and you're only reacting physically. What happens when we get back to San Francisco? When there are thousands of women ready to stand in my shoes?"

"The ones you threw away?"

"Don't make me hit you again."

"Where are they, anyway? Since I have to search the kingdom to win your hand."

She sighed. "On the boat."

"Yacht."

"Pretentious freak."

He ran a finger down the length of her nose. "Frigid bitch."

A smile played over her lips. "Don't goad me into disproving you. Man, you know every reverse psychology trick in the book."

"Majored in it in college."

"Not business?"

"That too, and literature."

"Wow. That couldn't have left much time for a social life."

"I wasn't there to party. I was there for the best education money could buy, and to get into the best business school I could."

"No drunken frat parties for you?"

"Not enough. You?"

"I planned the ones for my sorority, so I was in charge of setup and tear-down. But I liked it when everyone was having a good time." She tried to sound nonchalant, but didn't quite succeed.

"You should do that, plan parties. I don't expect you to be sitting home, waiting for me. I want you to have your own life, your own successes. You could go into business for yourself if you want."

"Maybe." She yawned.

"No matter what you decide, Heather. You set aside that dream for me, and I want to give it back to you. No matter what happens with us, I'll support you in that."

"I know." She reached her hand for his cheek, and he stiffened, unsure. "If we're going to be together, you have to let me touch you."

He reached out, resting his hand on her lace-covered hip beneath the warmth of the blankets. "Says the woman with the no-sex-in-a-bed rule."

"I'm afraid to touch you. You don't have a middle ground between friends and lovers."

"There isn't one." As if it had a mind of its own, his hand drifted around, cupping her rump.

"There is, Curtis. That's what marriage is. That middle ground that joins them both. I want to be able to hold your hand and not have you take it as an invitation."

He removed his hand, rolling onto his back.

"Or a rejection."

"Then you need to say what you mean."

"What did you think this would be like? How did you see us together?"

"However you wanted."

"That is a non-answer. When you thought up this scheme, how did you see it playing out?"

"I don't know."

"Were you planning on seducing me? Did you assume separate bedrooms? Jolly holly sticks, Curtis. Our first kiss was going to be in front of dozens of people and you didn't even blink an eye."

The deep breath he pulled in was filled with the apples-and-cinnamon scent of her. Not helping.

"I don't believe you. You see every strategic move five steps ahead in your mind. What did you see?"

"I didn't." She was right, he always did, and being with her had been a strategic move, hadn't it?

"You put me in a separate bedroom at your house."

He heaved a heavy sigh. "Did you see my bedroom?"

"Yes."

"I hate it. All black. Yours is better."

"Mine is pink."

"Better than black."

"So you planned on sharing my bedroom?"

"Maybe." Okay. Her falling asleep and shutting up would be great right now. He should have gone with that. He didn't like thinking about why he'd chosen her, why he'd gone so far with the plan. He had a sneaking suspicion he knew, and he did not like what that meant.

"Why?"

"What do you want me to say here, Heather? You're backing me into a trap. If I say I planned on sleeping with you, you think I'm treating you like a whore. If I say I didn't, you'll be offended. The truth is I didn't think of it beyond making you comfortable to make your own decision. You are my friend, if you wanted it to be more, that was your choice."

"So if I choose to sleep in the same bed, without sex, that's what will happen."

He groaned. "Woman, you are the master of manipulation."

"No, I learned from the master."

Chapter Twelve

Heather angrily swirled around the edge of sleep, her mind racing in opposite directions. Curtis was everything she wanted, and nothing she needed. He wouldn't even try to be more. She had to accept him as he was, or let the entire dream go.

She didn't even need to ask if he'd ever been in love, if someone had hurt him and it was that fear holding him back. He'd never even opened himself up to the possibility. She was sure she wasn't the first woman to fall in love with him, never to have it returned. Just as she knew she wouldn't be the last.

Nothing went that deep with him. Even this, the failure of their relationship, wouldn't be internalized with him. He'd think of it as a bad decision and write it off, while she would never really get past it. She'd always wonder if there was something she could have said, done, to open him up, let him out of his cave. Even though she knew he didn't have any desire to climb out of the hole on his own.

Beside her, his breath had deepened, growing slow and even, lulling her to relaxation. How could she love him so much, so completely, and he not feel anything?

Her hand reached for him, touching his warm chest, the fine hair tickling her palm. With each slow breath he took, her hand rose and fell, the tension in her body dissolving.

He wasn't Prince Charming, but she wasn't Cinderella either. Cinderella chased the prince as her escape, ran out of shame that he'd find her unworthy. That might have been her initial attraction to him, but she fell in love with the man who wanted to make the world better one project at a time, the man who overpaid his housekeeper and would cancel almost anything if his mother needed to have lunch. Heather knew the score, knew now what Curtis expected of their relationship. It wasn't all she hoped for, but it was far more than she expected a few days ago.

It wasn't enough to build a marriage on, but maybe in a few years it would be. If not, she wouldn't have to live with the regret of not trying. She'd circled back to the hopefulness from which all her troubles began, and yet, she was more optimistic it would work out this time. He liked her, supported her, called her a friend—that was more than a relationship of convenience. Wasn't it?

Curtis sucked in a sharp breath, startling her into removing her hand. In his sleep his brows furrowed together, his mouth moving. She watched as he twitched and twisted, his hands pulling at the covers.

"Don't," he pleaded, his voice a whisper. "Stop."

She turned towards him, unsure of waking him too quickly from his dream.

"Come back." The murmured words were hard to make out. "Don't leave."

"Curtis?" She tentatively placed her hand on his chest, his heart hammering beneath her palm.

"Heather?" He didn't open his eyes, just reached blindly for her. "Don't run, don't leave me." Wrapping an arm around her waist, he pulled her snug against him, nestling his head into the curve of her neck.

Her heart in her throat, she held him close, kissing his head as she smoothed his hair. "It's okay. You caught me."

By the end of the week, they'd agreed on a design plan for the house, worked through a timeline, watched the sun set every night, and made love on every available surface in the entire mansion. Heather found it quite a shame they'd be removing the lavish master bath to make way for guest suites, but after this morning in the shower, she knew Curtis's bathroom at home would have to be redone. Two showerheads was the only way to go.

With a naughty giggle, she pulled the lasagna from the oven, trading it quickly for the garlic bread. She loved trying on this life. How could she not? A big, beautiful house, stylish new designer wardrobe, and spending every moment with the most irresistible man in the world. Well, the western U. S., at least. There had been a poll.

Giggles turned to laughter as she rummaged through drawers for silverware. Last week she never would have guessed she'd share such steamy sexual chemistry with Curtis, or have so much in common. From their love of classic books, to their penchant for 1990s sitcom reruns, and undying affection for ice cream, she'd been seduced by him in every way.

It terrified her to think of how close she'd come to throwing away the opportunity to be with Curtis by running. She'd learned her lesson. From now on she'd state her case with him plainly instead of being awed by his heart-stopping magnetism. Well, not too awed.

Butter and garlic wafted to her nose, reminding her of the bread. She pulled it from the oven and set about plating their dinner, checking the window to make sure she still had time. Eating dinner with the sunset as a companion was addictive, and not something she wanted to miss. Who knew how often they'd be able to manage it once they got back into the city?

Once they got home he'd be working, and soon, so would she. They could meet up at cozy restaurants, steal quick moments before he headed back to the office and she headed home. In the dark they'd meet up in bed. Her no-sex rule had been thrown out the morning after she instigated it, but it had served its purpose well. He felt something, and even if he didn't know what it was, it was something they could build on.

A strange bit of serendipity that proved it would all work out eventually. He'd felt their connection, and even if it was unconsciously, it's what made him choose her, and it's what had him giving her another chance. That the sex was phenomenal didn't hurt.

Another smug giggle and she stepped to the terrace, expecting to find Curtis waiting as he had been all week, but she was alone as she put down the wine and set the table. She poured the wine, lit the candles, and stepped back, soaking in her perfect setting.

Maybe he was just empty, and if she filled him up with enough love and romance, he'd be able to give it back to her. She had enough romantic fantasies to keep them busy for the first few years, at least. By the time she made it back inside to collect their dinner plates, she was bursting with self-satisfied laughter.

"You seem to be enjoying yourself." Curtis stepped into the kitchen, a vase full of roses of every color in his hands and a newspaper tucked under his arm.

"Did you leave?"

"I wanted to bring you flowers." He pressed a quick kiss to

her cheek as he passed by, the warm scent of his cologne following him.

Her heart beat faster. He'd brought her flowers. It definitely put a swish to her hips as she carried the plates outside. Right up until she saw him seated at the table, the newspaper open and blocking his face from view.

"Thank goodness that country singer adopted a baby from Malawi. Though, once reporters tire of trashing her lack of parenting skills, they'll be back after us."

Heather cleared her throat, moving the vase to a side table. When she took her seat, the paper hadn't moved. She cleared her throat again. Still nothing.

"Curtis? Put the paper down."

He turned down a corner. "I've had nothing but internet news all week."

"That newspaper has a website that carries most of its content, and you have the news channels on every morning while you do too many sit-ups."

"The internet here is dial up. It drives me crazy."

"You're in the middle of a lake, Curtis. Sorry there is no Ethernet connection."

"Apology accepted." He had the nerve to smile before he went back to reading the paper.

Heather lifted a tapered candle, lighting the edge of his newspaper. She counted to four before he noticed, threw the thing to the ground and stomped it out.

"What the hell?" His foot still on the paper, he stared back at her, blue-green eyes flashing.

"Stop hiding behind a newspaper."

"For crying out loud, I'm not hiding behind anything," Curtis grumbled, sliding into his seat.

She looked down at the black-tinged newspaper, color tabloids peeking out from beneath. She bent down, pushing aside the paper to find three of those rags. Curtis grabbed them before she had a chance.

"You paid money for tabloids?" She clenched her fists, wondering what he was trying to hide.

"I wanted to know what we'd be dealing with when we got back."

"And?"

"Nothing we can't handle." Oh, that fake smile. It made her want to scream.

"Don't work me over like one of your clients."

"Heather—"

She stood, pushing her chair in.

"Where are you going?"

"Into town, to find out what you think you need to keep from me."

"And how do you plan to get there?" Curtis stood, rounding the table, the papers curled into a tube in his hand.

"The boat." She lifted her chin, meeting his gaze and holding it.

He rolled his eyes. "Yacht, and you don't know how to drive it."

"Think of your repair bill if I can't figure it out."

He shook his head, laughing as he pulled out her chair. "I really thought you'd be easier to handle."

"I don't care to be handled."

"That's not what you said this morning." He waggled his brows, reminding her of their exploits in the shower. Not that it could be helped. Between the showerheads and him, naked, no woman could resist.

With a huff of breath she snatched the papers from his hand and turned for the house. He caught her around the waist, pulling her back against him.

"If I don't get to read them without you, you can't read them without me. And we should wait until after dinner. You might lose your appetite."

She spun as he loosened his grip. "Why? What do they say?"

"Nothing true, but this is your first foray into tabloid journalism."

She shook her head. "No, I've been in them three times since the engagement was announced."

"Fine then, champ. If you think you can take it." Returning to his side of the table, he sat down, taking a long draw from his wineglass and refilling it.

Parking herself in her chair, she unrolled the tube, her eyes scanning the front page. A celebrity-relationship guru was involved in a sex scandal, the country singer and her adorable Malawian baby, reality-star-sex-tape debacle, and there she was. *Runaway Bride Plastic Surgery Nightmare.*

"Told you so."

She looked up, her eyes heavy with tears as she flipped through the pages to her story. "I haven't had plastic surgery."

"I know. I've checked you over thoroughly." He smiled wide, his grin bright in the waning light.

Ignoring his attempt to help, she looked down at the before picture, one of her rushing out of a coffee shop. She'd always thought black was slimming, but not in that photo. The after came from the photo shoot, after hours of professional support.

She looked like a completely different person. Still her, but without her glasses and with a face full of makeup and a head full of curls she did look like she'd had a lot of work done.

Had she really changed so much? She set that paper aside and looked through the next one. More humiliation was in store with a story claiming to be authenticated by her former boyfriend that the two had been having an affair and she was now pregnant with his child.

The tears started to choke her as she fought them. Her parents must be so disappointed. She didn't want to look anymore, and yet she couldn't help herself from wiping her eyes with the back of her hand so she could scan the last paper.

Frye's Bride Holding Out For More Money. She huffed, trying to get her mind off the ugly pictures, and betrayal by a man she used to care for.

"I don't want any money."

"Are you done crying?" He pulled the papers from in front of her.

"No," she choked, her throat hot and tight. "I can't believe this."

"It's not real, Heather. And it's much better than I expected. Kendra has been able to hold off a lot of it."

"How could it be worse?" She sniffed, wiping her eyes as the tears kept coming, rolling down her cheeks and dripping from her chin. She tried to stamp them down, but they refused to be swayed. Finally, she grabbed her napkin and covered her face, letting them out, her body shaking with the sobs.

"You know I don't know what to do when you're like this. These really aren't bad. None of them have any truth, so they'll go away faster. If we get married and start living a normal life, it will all go away."

Setting her elbows on the table, she took deep breaths

through the napkin, trying to get a hold of herself. Whenever she came close, her parents' faces swirled before her, the shock and letdown plain in their features. They'd raised their girls to be moral and upstanding members of the community. Not fodder for trash. And how had she ever trusted a man who could sell their relationship for a few dollars, turning what had been good once into garbage?

"Heather, calm down. There is no story in people who work hard and get along. We gave them something to pick at."

He hadn't, she had. She'd done this to herself, to her family. Her stomach twisted, acid burning.

"I can't marry you. You don't even want to love me." She pulled the napkin away, drying her face and blinking into the orange sunset. The sky was fuzzy to her right. "Just perfect. I lost a contact."

"This happened because it was a slow news week, not because of anything you did." He dropped the papers to the floor of the terrace. "We'll schedule laser surgery for your eyes as soon as we get back."

"Excuse me?"

"So you can see without glasses. It's amazing. You'll love it. No fumbling for glasses when you wake up in the morning, or getting something stuck in your lenses. The surgeon who did mine has an amazing success rate."

"I don't want someone cutting my eyeball." She kept blinking, turning her head to see him with her good eye.

He reached out, taking her hand. "I know it is scary, but he is the best in the business. I wouldn't trust anyone else with you."

"Why?" *Tell me you love me and this will all stop mattering so much.*

"I don't ever want to do anything to hurt you. And I wouldn't want anything to happen to your pretty green eyes." His thumb rubbed over the back of her hand before he released it, returning to his side of the table.

He'd never done anything to hurt her on purpose, but he knew she wanted things he couldn't give, and yet he still wanted her.

"Celebrities shouldn't adopt. It becomes such a circus."

She turned to watch him tucking the tabloids inside what was left of the charred paper.

"What are you talking about?"

"The country music star who has reporters scampering all over Africa for pictures of orphans."

"What's wrong with her adopting?" Heather wiped the last of her tears from her flushed cheeks. "She certainly has the resources to care for a child, and agencies put prospective parents through rigorous interviews."

"It's not her, exactly. All that child's life he'll be her *adopted* son."

"The press doesn't say that about you."

"That's because my father didn't enter politics until after they adopted me. If it was before, it would be my disclaimer."

"That's ridiculous. Any parent who is willing should be able to adopt."

"This isn't like your family, Heather. Celebrity children are photographed and chronicled, they aren't allowed to be kids. Adopted children have it hard enough." He took a swig of his wine, his fork playing with his dinner.

"What are you talking about?"

"Feeling abandoned, worthless, not good enough."

She reached for his hand. "Oh honey, not all adopted kids

feel that way. That wasn't what happened with you or with me."

He snatched his hand from hers, reaching for his fork. "Maybe not with you."

"The Fryes chose you as a child, not some baby they were rolling the dice with. You are fantastic and they wanted you to be a part of their family."

He leveled his gaze at her. "Let's not do this."

"You would never want to adopt?"

"What? To return the karma? No thanks. I'm not cut out for parenting in any form."

Her stomach tightened, her future narrowing until it was no longer the one she wanted. "You don't want to have children someday?"

"No." He chuckled, shaking his head. "I'm going to do the world a favor and end my blood line once and for all."

"Why?" She'd known people who didn't want children, but the desire had always been so strong in her, in her whole family, she didn't understand it.

"Heather, my father murdered someone. I don't want to pass those genes on."

She bristled, her blood running cold. "Mrs. Rutledge said he ran the drunk driver who killed your mother off the road."

"In a high-speed chase through town, with the lights of his patrol car flashing, while he was high."

"I'm not saying it was right, but it's not like—"

"You don't know anything about it. I'm not risking passing on his tendencies, genetic or otherwise. I'm not having kids. End of conversation."

She swallowed hard, bile burning her throat. "You don't want to have kids because of what your father did?"

"It's one of the reasons, yeah. More people should refuse to pass on violent traits."

Her head pounded, each beat of her heart pushing blood through her body, swollen with hurt and anger. "We are not the victims of our parents' wrongs. If my birth mother hadn't believed that I wouldn't be here now."

She stood, squeezing her hands into fists to keep them from shaking, but it didn't help her quivering voice. "I'll have children one day, not with you, someone who might look at them and see the men who raped my mother. When she learned she was pregnant, she thought everything good and pure in her that shattered that night had come together and created me. Not the violence, but the innocence she lost. I was her innocence handed back to her, and she found a situation for me where I could have all the things she couldn't give me.

"I am not responsible for someone else's wrongs, and I won't be with someone who thinks I am."

He stood as she stepped to the door. "Heather, that is not what I am saying."

She stood in the doorway, looking at him and the bright pink of the sunset beyond. "You don't hate yourself for what he did? Because that's what I just heard."

"They are two very different situations."

"No, they aren't. You are punishing yourself for something he did, and I won't let you punish me too."

"I wouldn't." He stepped closer, his eyes pleading for understanding. But this was the one area she could never back down on because it would change how she saw herself. "You don't understand, he raised me, he did things—"

"What about the Fryes? They adopted you because you were so wonderful."

"I don't know why they adopted me." He pushed his hair back off his forehead.

"You never asked?"

"Not once." He met her gaze and held it. "I'm not passing judgment on you, but I'll never have children."

"And I will." Perfection faded around her, the sky darkening as the sun dipped below the horizon. "I should get my things and go back to shore now." Her chest felt hollow, shrinking in on itself as her hopes withered inside.

"What?" He blinked a few times, shaking his head. "Why?"

"We're done. This is fundamental, Curtis. Who you are and who I am can't coexist. I'll go back to my parents' and you can have my things from your house shipped there." She turned, stepping into the house.

He grabbed her arm, spinning her back around to face him. "You stay here and finish the project. I'll go." He released her arm, stepping back and drawing in a deep breath. "If you ever change your mind—"

"I won't." She turned from him, walking as quickly as she could through the house and up the stairs, so she could cry behind the safety of her bedroom door.

She'd been so wrong about him, about everything. A person who hated themselves could never love anyone. And Curtis Frye thought of nothing but business, even keeping her here to finish a remodeling project after she'd rejected his proposal. If she wasn't an emotional wreck, and technically unemployed and homeless, she might have refused. But she believed in the project, and she needed the job to get back on her feet now that this sordid chapter in her life was over.

Chapter Thirteen

Time slipped through his fingers. Almost three months now and he still hadn't come up with a solution. Curtis hadn't spoken to Heather since the night he left Sapphire Isle, but he knew the remodeling project on the house was nearing completion. She'd been in constant email contact, always going through the amazingly efficient assistant she'd selected for him.

All that time and he was still no closer to thinking of a way to get her back. Out of frustration he'd replayed their last conversation in his mind, tripping over her incredulous question that he'd never asked the Fryes why they adopted him. He doubted it would give him any clarity, but at this point desperation won out.

He entered the Fryes' Huntington Beach estate through the garage, skirting as much of the staff as he could. They always made things so formal, announcing his presence like he was some kind of prince. He knew they all liked the pretense, but it made him uncomfortable and he was already ill at ease.

Dahlia Frye spent most mornings in her study, returning phone calls, so he sought her out there. When he heard voices in the hall, his steps faltered. He did not care to have this conversation with an audience. At the door he paused, listening to see whom was speaking.

"Forever Family is my favorite cause, that's why it gets so much of my time." Dahlia's tone was perfectly polished, the epitome of class.

"You devote a lot of your time to adoption charities. Is this because one of your children is adopted?"

"I'm a firm believer in adoption and making it affordable for families. Cost wasn't a factor for us, but it does deter some families."

Curtis smiled at the graceful deflection.

"I can see how that would be. I was thinking of steering the piece towards a more personal angle, using your special experience with adoption. Which of your children is adopted?"

"You know, I can't recall."

The stony silence unnerved him. Was this reporter fishing for dirt on him, or was this interview for real?

"I take that to mean you'd rather we focus on your charity work?" The reporter let out a nervous laugh.

"I think that would be for the best." He listened for a few more minutes as his mother rattled off more facts on adoption than he had ever heard in his life, then knocked softly on the door before pushing it open. His mother's office was ornately decorated in creams and golds. She and the reporter sat in high-backed chairs in front of her desk, his mother's phone at her elbow.

"Mother, when you get a moment—"

"We're just finishing up," Dahlia said, her smile thanking him for the reprieve. "Curtis, this is Jane Morton from the *Chronicle.* She's covering the Forever Family auction on Saturday. Did you get my invitation?"

"Yes, but we can't make it."

"Curtis, this is very important to me." The authoritative

tone cut him.

He eyed the reporter clutching both a recorder and notebook at the ready, but decided it was worth the risk not to upset his mother. Kendra had decided it best not to issue a statement to contradict her original story about why there was a scene in the middle of a photo shoot. Heather had stage fright, and they would wed secretly and quietly when the attention died down. Even his parents had bought the cover.

"I know, but with Heather's surgery, she won't be up to it yet." Not that she knew he'd scheduled it, or had agreed to it.

"Surgery?" the reporter asked, clutching her tape recorder in her hand. "Is Miss Tindall all right?"

He knew better than to talk in front of a reporter. This whole situation had him completely off his game. He plastered on his best smile and turned to speak to the media.

"Heather is wonderful. She's getting her vision corrected, so she won't be up to going out for a few days afterwards."

"Oh, that's good to hear it's nothing serious." She clicked off her tape recorder and slid it into the bag at her feet along with the notepad on her lap. She stood to shake his mother's hand. "Thank you so much for your time, Mrs. Frye." She turned to Curtis. "My best to Miss Tindall. Keeping up with the eye drops helped me recover quickly."

"Thank you." He smiled, not at all surprised when the maid showed up at the door to show the guest out. Dahlia kept the house hopping with just a few touches to the buttons of her house phone.

"This is a surprise." Dahlia motioned for him to take the vacated seat. "Are things going well at work?"

Curtis nodded, getting as comfortable as he could in the straight-backed chair.

"And Heather?"

"Her project is almost finished."

"Good." Dahlia gave a curt nod. "I'd like to have lunch with her when she gets back."

That's just what he needed, his mother running interference. "I'm sorry we won't be able to make this event."

"I'm sure Heather won't mind changing the date of her surgery. It's elective, after all." Dahlia straightened her shoulders, not a single wrinkle on her turquoise silk blouse.

Curtis cleared his throat, leveling his gaze at her. "I am very proud of all you've done, but we won't be there. Your devotion to adoption causes has to do with why I came."

"Really?" Her cheeks lifted in a genuine smile. "Is Heather looking for something she can be involved in?"

"This isn't about Heather. This is about me."

Her perfectly arched eyebrows lifted.

Might as well get to the point. "Why did you adopt me?"

She blinked once. "Because we loved you."

"Why did you adopt?" He stared at her face, seeing the thinness of her skin for the first time.

"What is prompting this, Curtis? Are you and Heather considering adoption?"

"No. I don't want children."

Her eyes widened, their powder blue color shining. "Really?"

Clearing his throat, he tried to steer the conversation back on track. "Did you always plan on adopting?"

"Yes, I did."

"An older child?"

"Yes, Curtis. What is it you need to hear?"

"I don't know." He dropped his head into his hands. A fight about adoption had started this whole mess with Heather. He'd hoped his mother had some magical answer to solve everything.

"I always knew I would adopt. Time got away from me a bit when your brother and sisters were young, and so an older child made more sense for our family. And you slid in so perfectly. You are so smart and hardworking, so easy for everyone to fall in love with."

He lifted his head, hating the worried look in her eyes. "You weren't afraid?"

"Of what?" Her smile was warm, softening her surprise.

"That I'd be like him?"

She blinked. "Who?"

"My..." *Father* seemed the wrong choice, as if it discounted John. "Jason Curtis."

"Oh, Curtis, really. Jason was a good man—he just fell apart when Diana died. He lost reality completely."

"That was the drugs."

"Yes, he was self-medicating. Losing your spouse is a lot of pain to be in. But we never worried you'd have a problem with drugs. We were very clear with all of you what our expectations were."

"He killed someone. You never worried I might have..." What exactly?

"Not once. Mrs. Rutledge knew I'd wanted to adopt. The moment she introduced you to us, it all came together and felt right. Didn't you think so?"

"I don't know what I thought. What I think." He stood, crossing the room to stare out the window. The rolling expanse of manicured lawn held no answers.

He hadn't expected an ulterior motive, but it would have

been a crutch to hobble back to Heather on. Instead, he found he was adopted by good people, for all the right reasons. Staring into nothing, he realized he'd known that all along. He'd shut down long before he came here, and even all the decadence and opportunity around him couldn't bring him to risk feeling anything. He didn't think he deserved it, so he'd worked hard to earn all he'd been given, and it would never be enough.

He'd never feel whole, never have another chance with Heather unless he faced what had closed him off in the first place.

"You're going to have to tell him yourself."

Peter Hardy, Curtis's new assistant, was dancing along Heather's last nerve. "No, you are capable of relaying the message."

"Why should I? If you don't want the job, decline it. If you don't want the surgery, don't sign the consent forms. But I am done playing monkey-in-the-middle with you two."

She couldn't blame him. The poor man had been fielding the terribly civilized emails she and Curtis exchanged almost daily for the last three months. But she wasn't ready to talk to him. Most days she still thought she'd made the biggest mistake of her life when she let him walk away.

"You know what I'd do? Come down for the eye surgery, and tell him then."

"Tell him while I can't see?"

"You'll be fine. I slept for the first two days, and was partying by the weekend."

But where would she stay for the first two days? And why

had Curtis scheduled the surgery anyway? Sure, he'd said he wanted to help her get a new start no matter what, but she never planned on holding him to it, not after the way they'd left things.

She sighed, leaning back in the leather desk chair in the newly decorated office of the Sapphire Isle estate. Her work here was done. A dozen guest rooms, a commercial kitchen, fire codes up to standard—she'd changed every inch of the house into the perfect cross between bed and breakfast and luxury hotel. She'd loved every minute of it, except when the contractors neglected to realize everything had to be brought to the island by barge, and wanted nothing more than to do it all over again.

Golden City had offered her a project-manager position, but how much Curtis had to do with that she wasn't sure. And she didn't know if she could work with him. She had to stand her ground and stop being his answer for everything, but she wasn't sure she was strong enough to resist the magnetic pull of all they could be, if she'd only let a part of her dreams die.

She could only see one way to find out. Full steam ahead.

"Can you arrange for a car to take me home from the surgery on Thursday? And book a room at a hotel?"

"Listen, it is obvious you two had a row, but you can go home. He won't be there, his calendar is blocked off until Tuesday."

Well, that answered that question. Curtis didn't care to see her, he'd scheduled her surgery while he was away. It would give her the perfect opportunity to pack her things. And see Curtis face to face in private when he got back. Yes, by next week she'd see everything clearly.

✧

He pressed open the door, amazed at how heavy the door between his garage and mudroom could be. Every movement felt as if he were underwater, being pulled at by an inevitable undertow. He toed off the sneakers and pulled the sweatshirt over his head.

"Jason?" Mrs. Rutledge appeared in the shadows. "Have you eaten?"

He didn't know what he felt, but it wasn't hunger. "You've seen him every month. Why would you betray me like that?"

"Visiting your father in prison does not betray *you.*"

"You talked to him about me! He knows everything I've ever done, thought, felt—"

"No one knows how you feel, Jason. Most of the time we talked of Diana, and how she would have loved to see you grow."

"Don't bring my mother into this." He pushed his hand through his hair, hoping removing the sweatshirt was enough to get rid of the stench of despair that clung to him after he visited the prison. He'd smelled it all the way home.

He stepped around Mrs. Rutledge, entering the house and heading for the bar in the formal living room. He had never needed a drink so badly in his life. There were too many thoughts in his head clamoring for notice. Some of them had to be quieted, or he'd never make sense of anything.

"Did you find what you needed?"

His fingers tensed as they wrapped around the neck of the bottle of Scotch. Lifting it, he set the bottle on the bar with a clang and reached for a highball glass. "Some ice would be good."

"Did you find what you needed from your father?"

"I don't know what I need." He filled the glass halfway and took a healthy swig, delighting in the heat that slid down his throat, pooled in his belly. Now if it would only calm his mind.

"Yes, you do. You always have."

"I don't know what you are talking about." He took another drink, then stepped toward her. "I don't like that you never told me you saw him, or that you've kept him up to date on my life. He gave up that right, and you had no—"

"He isn't in prison for leaving you."

"He signed away his parental rights."

Her gray head shook. "Because the Fryes were a better option than foster care. Your mother wouldn't have wanted that, so he did what she would have wanted and gave you a home."

"She would have wanted me in *my* home." With his father, no matter the monster he became. Curtis's head spun, his stomach churned. He hated this out-of-control sensation. Refilling his glass, he marched through the darkened house, making his way to the den where he sank into a leather armchair.

"Do you think you're doing what she would have wanted?"

"Me?" He twisted in his chair so his gaze could follow her as she stepped to the couch, the leather creaking as she sat.

"You. You live your life in a quiet terror. She wouldn't have wanted that."

"Pray tell, what am I afraid of?" He took another swig, lacing his every word with sarcasm. "I had my fear of the dark beat out of me by the man you visit like it is a religion."

"You're afraid to feel anything. You're not even comfortable with the rage you feel now. You think he abandoned you, that I betrayed you, and so you'll drink until you are numb, fall asleep, and never speak of it again. That's why I was concerned when you got involved with Heather."

He straightened up, pointing a finger at her. "Don't!"

"I will, because no one else dares. If you are going to continue to shut that girl out, let her go."

"How dare you!" Anger flooded through him, speeding his pulse. To release the fury he hurled the glass at the opposite wall, the explosion doing nothing to calm him.

"You're cleaning that up, Jason. I am not here to mop up after you, I stay here to make sure you maintain a connection with someone. I'm afraid if something happens to me, you'll close yourself off completely."

He swallowed hard, watching the Scotch drip down the wall. Heather's words from their first night on the island echoed back to him. *If you would only let yourself feel something, anything, I think it would be for me.* He'd shut off all emotion for so long, it was hard to recognize any feeling anymore.

His lips were painfully dry as he opened his mouth. "She left me." The words spoken aloud punched him in the gut.

"So, bring her back."

"I'm trying. She wants things I can't give her."

"Won't. You can do anything you set your mind to if you stop being afraid."

"I'm not afraid! I don't know how to be the man she needs."

"You'll learn. Heather is a patient woman, she'll be willing to teach you." She stood and walked to his chair, leaning a hand on his shoulder. "As long as you are in love with her."

He chuffed. "The woman has a Cinderella complex. She thinks life is a fairy tale where everything is perfect. She expects to be happily married and have children, and for nothing to ever shake that world."

"Why would you have her compromise? Hope for anything less?"

"It's not reality. Things happen you can't prepare for."

"Dreams aren't real until you make them happen. How is it you can be so forward-thinking in business but so cynical about life?"

"You of all people need to ask that?"

She shook her head slowly, squeezing his shoulder before she released it. "Maybe that's a question you should ask yourself. If life is short, shouldn't you live it to its fullest? Accomplishments don't make a life, love does."

Her footsteps down the hall punctuated her statement. Curtis slumped in the chair, closing his eyes. He'd been searching everywhere for the reason why he'd walked away from Heather without a fight, but the answer had been with him all the time. He didn't keep her at arm's length because he was adopted, because his mother died, or because of what his father did. He held back because he was afraid to lose her, had been from the moment he learned she might take another job.

Heather broke down barriers to reach him in a way no one ever had, gave life to his emotions. But he couldn't take in the good without the bad. To love her was to risk losing his soul if something were to happen to take her from him. He didn't know what terrified him more, losing her or finding himself.

Chapter Fourteen

"Where am I?"

Curtis jumped from the chair and made it to the bedside in two steps. "Don't try to open your eyes."

He took Heather's hand as she tried to reach for her eyes, covered with plastic shields. "Is it over?"

"You've been home for three hours. Let me turn off the lights and put some drops in your eyes, then you can open them. Your tear ducts won't work for a day or two." So he had to keep her from crying the way she was wont to do. No talking about anything that mattered.

Which was fine. Ever since he saw her through the window of the operating theater, the urgency to fix everything had faded. Her presence soothed his soul, buffing out the jagged edges that snagged on all the reasons she was right to turn down his proposal, until he felt as calm and sure as a mirrored lake.

"Oh, I remember now. You were there. I thought that was the medication." She stretched catlike in the bed, then froze. "Did you take my pants off?"

"It can't be comfortable to sleep in jeans." He flipped the lights, the only illumination coming from the hallway. Sitting on the bed next to where she lay, he removed the plastic eye shields and placed a drop of saline in the inside corner of each eye. Her dark lashes fanned against her pale cheek. Remembering his initial reaction after surgery, he took both of her hands in his.

"Okay, go ahead and open them." Her eyes cautiously opened and her hands instinctively jerked to touch them. He held them firm. She blinked a few times, allowing the drops to wet her eyes.

"I'm in my room, at your house." She squeezed his hand tighter. "And I can see my name on my diploma on the wall. I couldn't do that *with* my glasses on."

"You're sobering up. Do you want something to eat? It's a good idea to have something on your stomach when you take your pain pill."

"It doesn't hurt, really. I mean, it's scratchy and tired like I've been staring at a computer screen all day, but I can handle it."

He had to laugh. Heather, being tough. "The medication helps you sleep and gives your eyes a chance to heal. You need to take it. Corneal tissue heals in twenty-four hours, so if you sleep today you'll feel fine tomorrow. Besides, you might change your mind about the pain when I have to do the drops. The steroid ones aren't bad, but the antibiotic ones sting like a mother."

"Is that why you're doing this? To torture me?" She smiled, looking about the room. "Aren't you supposed to be out of town?"

"I took a few vacation days. You should be fine by the weekend, but I wanted to be home just in case."

"You cleared your schedule to take care of me?"

He shrugged. "You would have done it for me. What do you want to eat? I have peanut butter and jelly or just peanut butter."

She wrinkled her nose. "Where is Mrs. Rutledge?"

He clenched his teeth to keep from smiling. Best not to let her know what he had in mind. "On vacation. So what will it be?"

"How about I take another pill, and you order Chinese sometime before I wake up again?"

"How do people do this on their own?" She hated how whiny her voice sounded. She clenched her fists and willed herself to open her eyes. She yelped as soon as she did, the antibiotic drops making her eye burn. "I hate this."

"I know, but this is the last day. The doctor said you're a model patient, and as long as there is no redness we'll switch to just wetting drops tomorrow. Let's do the other eye now."

"It hurts, and my eyes can't tear to wash it away."

"You tried that excuse on the doctor. Now open up."

He got her again, and she twisted her head off his lap, sitting up on the couch. Her eyes still stung as she opened them, peering at the black-and-white movie on the television. They'd spent the entire weekend tiptoeing around talking about anything important. She'd slept through most of it, which made ignoring the pink elephant in the room easier. But now that she was off the medication, there was nothing to hold back her racing thoughts.

Why had he done all this, arranged the surgery, taken time off, cared for her himself when it would have been infinitely easier to hire a nurse or ship her back to her parents? She couldn't figure it out, and whenever she asked he refused to talk of anything that might make her cry. And given her track record, she couldn't argue with him.

"The doctor said I was fine. You should go to work." Definitely. *Give me some room so I can think clearly without your pheromones invading my senses.*

"This is your first day without the shields. It's easier if I stay home, in case something goes wrong."

"The doctor said I could have stopped wearing those silly plastic things on Friday, but you had me looking like a bug all weekend."

"I didn't want anything to go wrong with your gorgeous eyes." He got up from the couch, kissing the top of her head as he made his way back to her bedroom to put away the drops.

With a resigned sigh, she pushed off the couch and followed him. She had to do this, and the sooner the better. Every minute in his presence made her want to rethink her decision. But she'd spent her whole life arranging perfection for other people, always claiming contentment at watching the perfect party go off smoothly when what she really wanted was to be the belle of the ball. She wanted it all, or nothing. Settling for watching from the sidelines was no longer good enough.

Strangely, he'd given her the confidence to stand up for herself. If she hadn't been able to stir a reaction in him, hadn't earned his trust and desire, she might have taken the pieces of a life he offered. But there was no point starting a puzzle when you knew pieces were missing.

"Curtis," she said, standing in the doorway. "You should go to work. I don't want you to watch me pack."

He turned slowly, leaning a hand on the footboard of her bed. "I don't want you to go."

"I know." She sucked in a breath, struggling not to get emotional. "I'm going to take a shower so I don't have to watch you leave, and I'll be gone before you get back from work."

"You can't drive all the way back to Weed. It will be dark soon and it wouldn't be safe. What if you have trouble seeing at night?"

"I'm not driving home, I'll fly. One of the reasons I came back was to bring you the SUV. It belongs to Golden City, and I don't work there anymore."

"You don't want to be a project manager? I have folders on all the projects I've been pondering. You netted a half-million on Sapphire Isle when I sold it to Golden. Do you want to use that to start a party-planning business?"

"I don't want your money, Curtis."

"It's your money. We could be partners. There is an estate on Hawaii I think we could convert. I'll get the file." He took a step towards the door.

"No. I can't work with you, Curtis. I'm still in love with you. That doesn't change overnight, if ever. Working together isn't healthy for me." Her eyes felt heavy, but there were no tears to shed.

On the other side of the door hung her bright orange terry-cloth robe. She reached around, snagging it, but not before he caught her arm.

"Use my shower. I threw the rugs and towels from yours in the washing machine before we left for your doctor appointment."

She quirked an eyebrow. "You can do dishes *and* laundry?"

"My family is rich, not spoiled." He shoved his hands in the pockets of his slacks. "Go take your shower."

With a quick nod, she retreated down the hall and into her own thoughts. Did she really have the strength to walk away from him again? Last time she'd been the one to end things, but he'd been the one to leave. Could she do it if he asked her to stay?

Inside Curtis's bedroom she furrowed her brow. All the furniture was pushed up against the far wall, covered with drop cloths. Where had Curtis been sleeping? She'd had her eyes covered at night, and he'd been there as soon as she stirred to put the drops in. Had he been sleeping in the chair?

Stepping farther into the room, she spied the master bathroom. Before, when she'd carried his clothes in and helped Mrs. Rutledge to hang them in his closet, there had been a closed door. Now, there was a plastered archway, leading into a tiled room.

The large marble tiles were cool and slick beneath her feet, taking her breath away as she flicked on a light and stared about the room. He'd transformed it into a copy of the bath at the estate, albeit on a smaller scale. The shower looked identical, with tiled walls, showerheads on either end and body jets to spray along the front and back. He'd made one improvement to the design, installing a hand-held showerhead as well.

Okay. So maybe he *had* been thinking about them while they were apart. She smiled as she shed her clothes and turned on the spray. He'd thought about how great their physical chemistry was, at least. But that hadn't been the problem. He wanted to live a life where he kept everyone at arm's length, and one that excluded becoming a parent—something she knew she needed to experience one day.

Not today, the naughty side of her mind teased as she stepped beneath the spraying water. The steam misting up moistened her eyes, making them feel almost normal as she closed them, letting the water stream over her face.

Just like with the clothes, he'd wanted to share with her a feeling he'd had. This time he got it right. She'd always be grateful to him for the way he helped her see herself as worthy of a whole marriage. Without their time together on the island, she might have been willing to subject herself to the contract. Knowing she was able to stir the passions and respect of a man like Curtis Frye, she'd realized she'd never be happy with less than everything.

"I want you to stay."

Curtis's voice shocked her so much she nearly forgot to move her head from the water before opening her eyes to find him standing in front of the shower.

"I've done a lot of work while you were away."

"I can see that. Can we do this when I am not so..." She waved her hands in front of her body, highlighting her nakedness.

"I'm not talking about the bathroom. I'm talking about me. And you're not half as bare as I am right now, believe me."

His hands went to work on the buttons of his light blue shirt. "I asked my mother why they adopted me. No revelations there. I didn't feel any different."

As he peeled off the shirt and tossed it to the floor she held up her hand. "Curtis, I don't know if this is the best idea."

"It's all I have. I know it might not be enough, but it is the best I can do." He dropped his gaze, staring at his belt as he undid it. "After I talked with her, I went and sat on my mother's grave. Still no answers. I only saw one option, and as much as I didn't want to do it, I went to see him."

Realization rocked Heather back against the cooler tiles of the shower wall. He'd gone to see his father. He'd been searching for answers the entire time they were apart. The shower hadn't been a bribe, he wasn't looking for an easy way out. He wanted to be whole as much as she did.

Curtis shoved his pants to the floor, leaning against the wall to peel off his socks. "He asked about you. He seemed to know why I was there." His lips twitched as he shucked his boxers and walked to the shower.

"Please?" he asked, holding out his hand.

She took it, pulling him into the shower and wrapping her arms around him so they stood skin to skin, warming each other from the front while the showers cascaded down their backs.

"I told him everything." He looked down at her, his blue-green eyes glassy with a sheen she knew wasn't steam from the shower. "He cried, and I tried not to. But he didn't have any answers for me either. And so I went to your room, and lay on your bed, and I..." He squeezed his eyes shut, pulling her tight against him.

Unsure how to stop his pain, she simply held on, letting him find the words again.

His hands stroked over her wet hair, then framed her face. "I'm afraid to lose you. I have been for a long time. I need for you to love me like I need to breathe. Tell me I haven't gone too far to get you back."

Reaching up, she brought his mouth to hers, kissing him softly. He answered with a fervor she remembered well, but it didn't answer any of her lingering questions.

"Why do you want me back, Curtis? Is it because you hate to lose? To save face with the media?"

His eyes widened in alarm as he loosened his grasp on her. "No. I was fooling myself when I asked you to pose as my fiancée. It didn't have anything to do with the magazine article. It started when I found out you'd been offered another job. I started rationalizing why I didn't want you to go, and I was so out of touch with my feelings, I didn't realize I felt something.

"I asked you to try on the life, but I was the one who fell for it completely. You seduced me into wanting everything you could offer, all of it."

"*I* seduced *you*?" She'd thought she was merely a piece in his game. If she affected him in the same way he did her, maybe she'd been right and he did feel something. Something intense enough to search deep into his soul for a way for them to be together.

"I'll never look at a swimming pool the same way again." His lips twitched into a smile.

She tried not to answer with a grin of her own. "What is it you want, Curtis?"

"I need to know I have you to come home to every day. I want to be your husband. A real one. I could be good at it. I've taken good care of you since the surgery, right?"

"Yes, you have, but I don't need to be taken care of, and that wasn't our problem."

"You're right. I needed to face the real reason why I didn't want children. It wasn't being adopted, and it wasn't my father's crimes. Without your pushing I never would have looked close enough to see that it wasn't having a child I was afraid of, but of shutting one out the way I do everything else, even of abandoning one."

"You would never—"

"Do what he did? Choose vengeance over dealing with life? It would be tempting." He framed her face again, kissing her softly this time. "I don't know how I'd live if you were gone. I've missed you so much, and you were only an hour away."

Hot kisses trailed across her mouth, over her jaw. Heat swirled through her body, already warm from the ministrations of the shower. Could she trust what he showed her, believe that actions spoke louder than words, or was she deluding herself again?

Trust. She had to trust him and his actions, trust herself and her feelings. "You know, if you never fill in the blanks, I write my own story."

"A fairy tale?" Laughter vibrated against her skin as his hands traveled down her body. "They always get married before they live happily ever after."

"You are like a broken record." She giggled as he lifted her off her feet, her back pressing against the tiled wall. "Okay, you convinced me."

"No, I'm not done convincing you yet." His hands grasped her hips and she squealed.

"You have to be. I could get pregnant."

He narrowed his eyes, touching his nose to hers. "What?"

"My birth control only lasted for three months. I didn't get another dose."

"Okay." He dipped his head, kissing her neck again, his wet hair brushing against her cheek.

"Not okay." She gripped at his shoulders.

"But you want a baby." He met her gaze, the incredulous look in his eyes making her smile.

"Not right now. You want a baby *now*?"

He shrugged his shoulders, shocking her to the core. Doubt evaporated into the steam rising around them. Unless he loved her, he wouldn't be willing to give them a child, not with the way he felt about family.

"You know what we could do instead?" She trailed her hand down his chest, where he caught her wrist.

"Make use of the condoms in the bathroom drawer?"

"Oh, thank goodness."

He flashed his megawatt smile and dashed out of the shower. Heather wrapped her arms around herself, feeling the happiness bubbling up from her toes to the top of her head. She'd always known some day her prince would come.

Epilogue

One week later...

Meet me on the beach to watch the sunset.

Heather read the note, scrawled in Curtis's scratchy script, and smiled. He knew just what to do to talk her into tackling the conversion of the sprawling Maui estate into their next project.

Situated on the north shore between a sprawling cattle ranch and a botanical garden, the house and its cottages were breathtaking. The site barely needed a facelift. Still, it would be a great investment property, especially if they could visit frequently and find that waterfall off the Honopi'ilani Highway again. And again.

With a naughty laugh, Heather looked toward the bed where she'd found the note. Sprawled across the duvet were a creamy silk gown and lei of pink flowers.

A thought struck her as she slipped into the dress and looped the lei around her neck. If she transformed the estate into a private wedding resort, it couldn't fail. Romance blossomed with the flowers on the island. The cottages made perfect accommodations for a collection of guests. And who didn't dream of getting married on a private beach, barefoot, with their toes in the sand?

Quite proud of herself, she found a pair of sandals that would be easy to slip off and made her way out of the house and to the beach. Humidity wrapped around her like a lover's embrace as she stepped outside, the sweet scents of plumeria and oleander dancing in the air. Pulling her hair over one shoulder, she took the path that wove through the seven cottages, taking mental notes as to which improvements could be made.

The grassy path dipped, the shrubbery clearing as the sound of the surf grew louder. She slipped off her sandals and started for the beach, the taste of salt sprinkled in the air.

Her toes touched sand and her heart stalled. On the beach stood her family, and Curtis's, everyone dressed in white. Except for a large man in a bold Hawaiian print shirt, holding a small black book, and a woman in a floral wrap dress already snapping pictures with a camera.

Catching sight of her, her father waved, prompting the small collection of people to do the same. The first tear fell before she could think. Without Curtis none of them would be here, and she wouldn't be able to see them if they were.

With confidence she walked to them, her family, or she guessed they all would be in a matter of minutes. Her footsteps faltered. *Where is Curtis?*

Shielding her eyes with her hands, she scanned the beach. The clip clop of hoof beats turned her around just in time to see Curtis and another man galloping down on her. She shrieked with laughter, the absurdity of her prince on a white horse making the scene dreamlike.

He hopped down a few yards from her. "Have you ridden a horse before?"

She shook her head, words having escaped her completely.

"Tomorrow then." He tossed his reins to the other man,

who turned both horses and made his way back up the beach.

Who needed words when body language could speak for you? Heather closed the distance between them, vining her arms around his neck and pulling him down to her as she rose up on her toes to meet him. She scarcely had time to enjoy the feel of his mouth on hers when he straightened back up and unwrapped her arms.

"I love you too, but you don't get to kiss me until after." He took her hand, tugging her to where their family had gathered.

She didn't hear a word of what was said. Her thoughts even muted the sound of the ocean. He loved her. She knew it before, but hadn't heard it. She stared at him as they stood in front of the man in the Hawaiian shirt, holding hands and smiling like crazy.

She'd been silly to think the words mattered more than the actions. If she'd just trusted what he showed her from the beginning, instead of getting hung up on the details, it wouldn't have taken half as long to get here.

"Heather." Curtis squeezed her hands, bringing her back down to earth.

"I love you." The words flowed like water from the falls.

"Yes, but will you marry me?" He smiled, tilting his head towards the officiant.

"I will," she said to Curtis, then repeated herself to the other man while their families laughed.

"So she can kiss me now?" Curtis asked, pulling her closer. "She's been waiting all afternoon."

The sun blazed in the distance, flirting with the sea. Time to get their feet wet. She pulled him down the beach with her until the waves lapped about their ankles.

"You may kiss your bride, Mr. Frye," she teased, brushing

her lips against his.

He kissed her with a savage passion that filled her with anticipation of the life to come.

About the Author

Jenna Bayley-Burke is a domestic engineer, freelance writer, award-winning recipe developer, romance novelist, cookbook author and freebie fanatic. Blame it on television, a high-sugar diet, or ADD; she finds life too interesting to commit to one thing—except her high school sweetheart and two blueberry-eyed baby boys. Her novels can be found online and in bookstores, as long as you live in the UK. Her short stories, both naughty and nice, are available online and in print anthologies.

To learn more about Jenna Bayley-Burke, please visit www.jennabayleyburke.com. Send an email to Jenna at jbayley@hotmail.com or visit her blog at http://jennabayley-burke.blogspot.com.

A stodgy lawyer butts heads with a free spirit. Let the mattress dancing begin!

Ready or Not

© 2007 Anara Bella

At first, Brianna Michaels' agreement to fill in as a bachelor party stripper sounds like a win-win situation. She's returning a favor to a friend, and earning some much-needed cash. But when she sees the man she's lusted after for years in the audience, baring all suddenly doesn't seem like such a hot idea.

Quinn MacRae stops the show—literally—when he reacts instinctively to protect Brianna and her reputation. Plus, it's nearly unbearable to see exactly what he's been missing. As an attorney with a prestigious law firm, he's sure of one thing. Brianna would hate living in his world. She's the last woman he should be lusting after.

But lust he does—with a vengeance.

Available now in ebook from Samhain Publishing.

LaVergne, TN USA
27 January 2011
214257LV00003B/24/P